# VIKING BOY

## TONY BRADMAN

*Illustrated by Pierre-Denis Goux*

WITHDRAWN FROM STOCK

**WALKER BOOKS**

This is a work of fiction. Names, characters, places and incidents
are either the product of the author's imagination or, if real, used
fictitiously. All statements, activities, stunts, descriptions, information
and material of any other kind contained herein are included for
entertainment purposes only and should not be relied on for
accuracy or replicated as they may result in injury.

First published in Great Britain 2012 by Walker Books Ltd
87 Vauxhall Walk, London SE11 5HJ

11

Text © 2012 Tony Bradman
Illustrations © 2012 Pierre-Denis Goux

The right of Tony Bradman and Pierre-Denis Goux to be identified as
author and illustrator respectively of this work has been asserted by them
in accordance with the Copyright, Designs and Patents Act 1988

This book has been typeset in Stempel Garamond LT Std

Printed and bound by CPI Group (UK) Ltd, Croydon, CR0 4YY

All rights reserved. No part of this book may be reproduced,
transmitted, or stored in an information retrieval system in any
form or by any means, graphic, electronic, or mechanical,
including photocopying, taping, and recording, without prior
written permission from the publisher.

British Library Cataloguing in Publication Data:
a catalogue record for this book is
available from the British Library

ISBN 978-1-4063-1383-3

www.walker.co.uk

MIX
Paper from
responsible sources
FSC® C020471

# FOR NICK, AND FOR TOM,
# WHO SHOWED ME THE WAY

# CONTENTS

*Three voices speak in the deep darkness*
*by the giant roots of Yggdrasil, great*
*tree of worlds, its colossal bulk rising*
*high into the sky above.*
*"Spin and weave..." says the first,*
*the oldest, voice of that which has been.*
*"A line of silver thread..." says the*
*second, voice of that which is now.*
*"One little snip ... and then you're*
*dead," says the third, voice of all that*
*which is yet to come.*
*The Three Sisters cackle, and their vast*
*web trembles. It stands around them,*
*endlessly tangled and knotted and*
*pulsing with life.*

*Sudden light in the darkness, a small*
*glowing pool like a shimmering mirror.*
*Three faces leaning over it, reflecting*
*the gleam, eagerly searching the ripples*
*for what they might see. Soon an image*
*appears on the surface.*
*"Who's that?" says the oldest, peering.*
*"Is it the boy, our chosen one?"*
*"It's him and no other," says the second.*
*"Happy as a dolphin leaping."*
*"He'll suffer before we're done," says*
*the third, and they cackle again. They*
*join bony hands and dance wildly round*
*the pool, chanting as they caper, their*
*hair like nests of snakes, their ragged*
*black cloaks whirling...*

*"Men's fates we weave from birth to death*
*We number each and every breath*
*We are the Norns who always win.*
*Now let this Viking tale begin..."*

# ONE

# MEN'S

# WORK

**GUNNAR WAS DOWN** by the sheep pens when he heard the rhythmic thumping of hoofbeats and the jingle of harness and weapons sounding distantly through the crisp autumn air. He frowned and looked up, along the track that led from the steading's gate

11

to the dark forest, then turned and ran to the long-house.

His parents were sitting together on a bench by the hearth, smoke from the fire rising to the hole in the thatch. A pot hung above the flames, and the smells of woodsmoke and stew wrapped themselves round him like the furs he slept beneath at night. They were laughing, and Mother was ladling stew into bowls.

Everybody said Gunnar and his father were as alike as two ears of corn, although Gunnar couldn't see it. They both had shaggy brown hair, but Father's hair and beard were flecked with grey. They both had hazel eyes, but Gunnar's were darker. And they both had strong features and broad shoulders, but Father was tall, and even at fifteen summers Gunnar was still half a head shorter. Mother's hair was golden, and Father said her eyes were the colour of the sea, changing from blue to green to grey according to the light, or her mood.

"Ah, here's our boy, just in time for supper as usual," said Father, grinning at him. Like Gunnar,

12

he was wearing a tunic and leggings and leather boots. Mother wore a green gown and a silver necklace, and she smiled too.

"I swear you could smell my stew from the other side of the mountains," she said.

"Riders in the forest," Gunnar said breathlessly. "Heading this way."

Father stood up, his smile gone. Mother's face clouded over.

"How many?" said Father, his voice steady, eyes fixed on his son's.

"Hard to say," Gunnar answered. "Six, maybe seven at the most."

"Who could it be?" said Mother, her hand on her husband's arm.

"We'll know when they get here," said Father. "It's probably nothing, but we'd better make sure there's a proper welcome, just in case. Ranulf! Arnor!" he shouted. Two men appeared from the shadows. "Get your hunting spears, and tell the others to do the same. Gunnar, fetch my sword."

Gunnar ran to his parents' curtained-off chamber

13

and raised the lid of the chest that stood at the end of their bed. It contained many things – clothes and furs, the best bowls and goblets. But lying on top was the sword Father had used as a young Viking, and in Miklagard as a soldier of the Greek Emperor's guard. It was in a wooden scabbard lined inside with sheep's fleece, the oily wool keeping the metal free from rust. An ivory hilt bound with age-darkened leather was topped off by a round pommel inlaid with gold and silver. The blade had a shallow groove running from hilt to tip, and was razor-sharp on both edges.

Now Gunnar lifted sword and scabbard from the chest, partially pulled the blade free, and held it up so the glow from the hearth could fall on it. Faint lines twisted and writhed in the metal, almost as if the sword were alive and the red firelight brought back memories of the day it had been born in some ancient forge's heat. Runes were carved on the blade, a cluster of spiky letters that spelled the sword's name – DEATH-BRINGER.

He pushed the blade back into the scabbard and

hurried outside. A crowd had gathered, the people of the farm coming out to see who the visitors might be. Gunnar made his way through them, the men talking in hushed voices, the women clutching their children, everyone uneasy, but curious as well.

Father was waiting with his men in front of the longhouse, Mother by his side. Gunnar handed him the sword and Father buckled it on.

"It's time you went indoors now, Helga," Father said softly. "And best take the boy in with you. This will be men's work."

"All the more reason for a woman to keep an eye on you," snapped Mother. "But you'd better do as your father says, Gunnar."

"No, I won't," muttered Gunnar. "If you're staying, I'm staying too."

"Would you listen to the pair of them?" said Father, rolling his eyes. "Maybe some day I'll find out what it's like to be obeyed by my family."

The men around him laughed nervously. Ranulf was staring wide-eyed at the gate, holding the shaft of his hunting spear as if he would never let it go, his knuckles white. Stout, balding Arnor stood beside him, chewing his lip.

"Here they come," Ranulf whispered. "They're in full war gear."

"I can see that for myself, Ranulf," said Father. Gunnar noticed him touching the small amulet of Thor he wore on a leather thong round his neck.

The riders thundered through the gateway and up to the longhouse, seven men on powerful, snorting horses. They seemed enormous in the fading light, the setting sun's rays glinting off their weapons, their shadows reaching out before them. They wore chainmail and helmets with holes for their eyes, and carried spears and round shields. Swords hung from their studded belts.

"I bid you welcome to my farm, Skuli, son of Eyjolf," Father said when the riders halted. "But I wonder why you're so far from home on this chill autumn evening, and why you're armed for war. If it's bad news you've brought, then I'd rather you stepped into the warmth of my hall and told me over supper."

"You have a good memory, Bjorn, son of Sigurd," said the leading warrior, jumping off his horse. He removed his helmet and smiled, his teeth white in a bushy black beard. "We met only once, and that was two years ago."

"How could I forget a face as ugly as yours?" said Father, smiling too.

"You're calling *me* ugly?" said Skuli. "I'd like to know how a man as ugly as you could have persuaded such a beauty to be his wife. So this is Helga."

Skuli cast his eyes over Mother, grinning at her, before turning his gaze back to Father. There was a ripple of muttering in the crowd by the longhouse, but Gunnar knew this was the sort of banter men liked to indulge in.

"I took pity on him, of course, daft girl that I was," said Mother. "Now if you two boys would care to stop playing games, I'd like to go inside and eat."

"Wit as well as beauty, eh?" said Skuli, laughing. "As it happens, I do have some news for you, Bjorn. And we'd be happy to accept your hospitality."

The two men shook hands the Viking way,

17

gripping each other's forearms, and they went in, much to everyone's relief, Skuli and his men leaving their weapons stacked in the porch, as guests should. Mother had the long tables put out and food and drink prepared, and soon the hall was filled with voices and laughter, flames leaping in the hearth. Gunnar sat near Father and Skuli and listened as they talked about many things – including, at last, Skuli's news.

"There's word a band of raiders is sniffing around," he said. "So I thought I ought to show myself – and warn the local farmers, of course. You have a fine holding. I would hate to see it looted and burned by a bunch of outlaws."

"That's good of you," said Father. Gunnar remembered they'd heard plenty of talk about Skuli recently. Their guest was a man with ambitions. He owned several farms, and some said he had fifty warriors at his beck and call. Some also said he had his mind set on becoming a jarl, perhaps even a king.

"Well, you know how it is, my friend," Skuli said. "I'd like people to think I'm a man who will help

18

them. Just in case I need help myself some day."

"Help to do what?" said Father, his eyes fixed on Skuli's, a slight frown on his face. "You're the richest and most powerful man in the district."

"And you're the most respected. Who knows what I couldn't do with a man like you by my side? Don't you want power and wealth too?"

Father smiled at him and shook his head. "I'm happy enough with what I have, and I want no more. I like a quiet life these days."

"Are you sure?" said Skuli, leaning forward. "I'd hate to think you might oppose me in what I aim to do, Bjorn Sigurdsson."

"You have nothing to fear from me," said Father, his voice steady. "So then," he went on, "what else can you tell me about these raiders?"

Skuli paused, studying Father's face, or so it seemed to Gunnar. At last Skuli smiled. "Not much more, in truth," he said.

"Well, thanks for the warning," said Father. "We'll post guards from now on. You can never be too careful."

The conversation moved on, Skuli boasting about great warriors he had known and battles he had fought in. Father said little. Later, as Gunnar lay down to sleep, he went over Skuli's stories in his mind, wondering if he would ever stand shoulder to shoulder with a band of warriors when he was a man.

In the forest, wolves howled and shadows gathered in the darkness.

# TWO
# FIRE IN THE NIGHT

SKULI AND HIS men left the next morning. In the days that followed, Father arranged for guards to be posted, the men of the farm taking it in turns to keep watch. But nothing

21

happened, and after a while Gunnar forgot Skuli's warning – until one night when he woke with the smell of smoke in his nostrils.

It always smelled of smoke inside the longhouse, but they usually let the hearth fire burn down at night, and the smell shouldn't have been so strong. There was a little light coming from the fire's embers, and Gunnar could make out the shapes of sleeping servants round the hearth. He slid out from beneath his furs, raised his eyes – and his heart jumped. A tongue of flame was licking at the underside of the thatch, tendrils of smoke curling from it like snakes.

"Father, Mother, wake up!" Gunnar yelled, yanking back the curtains to their chamber. "The roof is on fire!" His parents were soon out of bed and looking up at the flames, the servants waking too and crowding round them.

"What do you want us to do?" said Arnor, appearing from the shadows.

"Get everybody outside," said Father. "Then start filling pots with water. We can probably save most of the roof if we get it damped down."

Arnor started pushing everyone towards the porch. He unbarred the door and opened it, but he didn't get far. Gunnar heard a humming sound and Arnor grunted, falling back into the arms of the people behind him. Arnor was dead, three arrows in his chest, a dark bloodstain spreading across his tunic.

Gunnar felt sick, hardly able to believe what he was seeing. Father stepped over Arnor's body, slammed the door shut and banged the bar down into place again. He quickly moved to one of the small windows in the wall, pulled open the shutters a crack and peered out. More arrows thunked into the wood of the longhouse.

"Who brings fire in the night and murder to my hall?" he roared.

There was no answer for a moment. Gunnar glanced up and saw the flames spreading. His mother grabbed him and moved him towards another window, then turned to him with a finger across her lips and carefully pulled the shutters open.

"We are the Wolf Men, bringers of fire and slaughter," a voice outside growled at last. "And we will give you a choice of endings."

Gunnar peered through the window and felt his blood go cold. A line of fierce-looking warriors stood facing the longhouse beneath the star-filled sky. There were perhaps thirty of them, most wearing leather jerkins, only a few in chainmail. But they all wore wolf's head helmets, and carried spears decorated with wolf tails and shields painted with pictures of snarling wolves.

Several held torches, the flames casting shadows that danced, and three had war bows, arrows notched and ready to be fired. There were dogs too, five massive beasts straining at their leashes, their jaws parted to reveal white fangs, their wild eyes reflecting the red light of the torches.

Another man stood in front of the line, and Gunnar realized he was the one who had spoken, their chief. He wore a mail shirt, but his head was bare, his grey-streaked black hair hanging to his shoulders. He wore a long wolfskin cloak, and the blade of his un-sheathed sword glinted in the starlight. A couple of Wolf Men with torches moved up beside him.

"A choice?" said Father. "That's generous of you,

24

but I'm sure I can guess what it is. Stay in here and burn, or come out with my gold and silver and anything else worth stealing. Then you'll cut my throat anyway, and probably kill everybody else too. Or sell them as slaves, which is worse."

"I can see you know how this works," said the chief. "But we're not as bad as that. I'll let the women and children and servants live, and maybe only sell a few. And maybe we'll even let you fight for your life. We could do with some fun, eh, lads?" His men laughed and yelled their wild war-whoops and howled like wolves. "Your night guard wasn't much of a challenge."

The chief nodded, and another of his men threw something round onto the ground. It rolled slowly towards the longhouse, and Gunnar realized it was Ranulf's head, the eyes wide open, the hair darkened with blood.

"Glad to hear you'll give me a chance," said Father. "I'll think about it."

"Don't think too long," said the chief. "I can be very impatient."

Gunnar saw him nod, and the two men beside him ran forward and threw their torches high into the air. The flames flapped and hissed as the torches spun end over end and thumped onto the roof, and the Wolf Men cheered.

Mother hurried over to Father with Gunnar. "What are we going to do?" she said. "We don't have much time... The roof isn't going to last long."

As if to underscore her words, one of the roof beams groaned and crashed down in a shower of sparks. Everyone ducked, and the longhouse filled with acrid smoke and small, floating pieces of burning thatch. Father pulled his wife and son closer to him. "I can't save everybody," he whispered, his face anguished. "You two have to come first."

Then he turned to the others and spoke loudly so they could hear him above the sound of the flames. "It looks like we have no choice. Out you go, quickly now..." He didn't wait to see whether they obeyed him, but hurried his wife and son back to the curtained-off chamber.

"I think we can make a hole in the wall here,"

Father said. "Help me." He pushed hard at one part of the wall, and Gunnar and Mother pushed too. Soon the turves were loosening. "We'll need to be ready. Put on some warm clothes, but nothing that will stop you running. We'll make for the forest."

Gunnar and Mother busied themselves with finding clothes and pulling on boots. "We're ready," said Mother at last. She glanced up, and Gunnar followed her gaze. The fire had reached the thatch above them, and smoke billowed through the curtains.

Father had pulled on a thick tunic and strapped his sword on his hip. "Here we go," he said, giving the wall a kick. The turves shifted and buckled then collapsed, folding in on themselves, and a hole appeared.

"Come on, Gunnar," said Mother. They rushed out together – and ran straight into one of the Wolf Men. "To me, lads!" he yelled. "I've got a couple here!"

Suddenly Gunnar heard a hissing sound and saw a bright gleam sweep clean through the raider's neck. Gunnar blinked with the speed of it, then saw the Wolf Man's head bounce away across the grass. The man's body seemed to realize something final had

27

occurred, and slowly crumpled to the ground.

Father stepped over the corpse, Death-Bringer shining in his hand. Behind him the flames from the burning longhouse leaped into the sky.

"That's for Arnor," he hissed. He turned to Gunnar and Mother. "Run!"

It was too late. Gunnar heard snarling and saw the dogs come racing round one end of the longhouse, followed by a dozen Wolf Men. Father took the shield of the man he had killed, Mother grabbed the spear from the dead man's hand, and they both turned to face the onslaught. Gunnar picked up a rock from the ground and stood between them, wishing he had a better weapon.

The first of the raiders reached them and also raised his spear, but Father brushed it aside with the shield and let the man run onto Death-Bringer, the blade piercing him through. Father yanked Death-Bringer out of his guts. "And that's for Ranulf," he hissed, seeking out the next opponent.

Two more Wolf Men and the first of the dogs attacked together. Father took one warrior low,

Death-Bringer slicing through his legs, and the other high, with a stroke that almost severed the man's spear arm, finishing both with thrusts into their chests. Mother dealt with the dog, skewering the snarling animal on her spear as it leaped, the others skidding to a halt just out of range, growling and showing their fangs. The rest of the warriors stopped as well, spreading to form a circle round Gunnar and his parents. Gunnar could see the archers among them, arrows notched in their bows.

Father stood before his wife and son, covering them with the shield, watching the Wolf Men. Gunnar's heart pounded as if it were about to burst through his ribs. All three panted in ragged gasps, their breath a cloud in the cold night air.

"Why have they stopped?" whispered Mother.

"They're waiting for me," said a deep voice.

Suddenly two more men appeared and walked into the circle. Gunnar saw that one was the Wolf Men's chief. But then he drew in his breath sharply.

The other was Skuli.

# THREE
# GUNNAR'S
# OATH

GUNNAR'S MIND WAS a whirl of hope and fear and confusion. Was this all a terrible mistake? Had Skuli come to save them? Then he guessed the truth, and felt a wave of hatred for Skuli sweep through him.

Skuli and the Wolf Men were linked – and judging by the way the Wolf Men's chief was hanging back behind him, Skuli was the man in charge.

"I'm impressed, Bjorn," said Skuli. He stood with hands on hips, a tall, dark figure outlined against the flames consuming the longhouse. He wore a helmet and chainmail, but carried no shield, and his sword was still sheathed. "I've heard stories about how good you used to be in battle, and now I can see they were true. It's a shame you and I were never shield brothers."

"I always chose my shield brothers carefully," said Father. "I would never have fought alongside any man who lied as you have, Skuli."

"I told no lies," said Skuli, grinning. "I just didn't mention that the raiders I warned you about are my own men."

"You're a coward," said Mother. "The kind of scum who gets others to do his dirty work. I should never have let you inside my home."

"That's a bit harsh, Helga," Skuli said. "I'm happy to do my own dirty work when I have to. But why

31

keep a wolf and howl yourself? It was easier to get Grim and his lads to make sure your husband wouldn't be a problem. This is all his fault. I offered him a chance to join me, and he turned me down."

Just then Gunnar saw the Wolf Men's chief – or Grim as he now knew he was called – give a signal to the archers. They spread out, making it impossible for Father to keep Mother, Gunnar and himself protected by the shield at the same time. Mother pulled Gunnar to her and he waited for the arrows to rip into his flesh. But that didn't happen, and Father lowered the shield.

"Let's not be hasty here, Skuli," he said. "Maybe we got off on the wrong foot the other day. I'm a reasonable man. Surely we can talk some more..."

"The time for talking is over," said Grim, scowling. "You made sure of that when you killed four of my men. Skuli, we need to finish this."

"I know," said Skuli, almost sadly. "Sorry, Bjorn," he added.

"*NO!*" screamed Mother, and Father sprang at Skuli, Death-Bringer raised. Grim nodded at his archers. Two arrows thudded into the shield, but the third struck Father in the chest. He staggered and dropped the shield, and Grim stepped forward to take a swing at him. Father parried the blow with Death-Bringer, the swords smashing together with a mighty *CLANG!*

Mother leaped forward, aiming her spear at Grim, but one of the Wolf Men grabbed her, making her drop it. She kicked and screamed, but there was nothing she could do. Gunnar stood paralysed, letting the rock fall from his hand, watching as Father sank to the ground and onto his back.

Skuli walked over and looked down at him. "Cut his throat!" yelled another of the Wolf Men, the rest baying their agreement. Skuli shook his head.

"No need," he said. "The moment of his doom is near."

Mother shook off the Wolf Man holding her and ran to Father, kneeling next to him and sobbing, and Gunnar joined them. If only he was a man, a warrior like Father! If only he had been able to stand with him and take his share of the fighting! He was his father's son, and to his shame he had done nothing.

Mother moaned and leaned over Father. He still held the hilt of Death-Bringer in his right hand. "Don't you dare die!" she said. "I won't let you!"

"Helga… Gunnar…" whispered Father, his breath coming in gasps, his chest heaving, his tunic darkening with the blood pulsing up round the arrow. His face was already deathly white, like that of a ghost. He squeezed his wife's hands, moved his head so he could see Gunnar. "I'm sorry…"

Gunnar looked into his eyes, but they changed, locking into stillness, a last sigh escaping from Father's mouth. Mother howled and Gunnar buried his face in Father's neck, the skin cool and smelling of smoke. He felt Father's amulet beneath his hand and gripped it, enormous sobs surging through him.

"Take the woman and the boy to the front of the longhouse," Skuli said. "Bring the body too, so the rest can see it."

Gunnar felt rough hands grab him. He kicked and fought and tried not to let go of Father or the amulet on its leather thong. Two raiders pulled him

34

away, snapping the thong and leaving the amulet clutched in Gunnar's fist. Mother was dragged away too, screaming something he couldn't make out. The longhouse burned beyond her, red flames leaping into the sky.

Gunnar and Mother were thrown down. Father's body was thrown down as well, just a few feet away from them, and Death-Bringer tossed on the ground beside him. The Wolf Men danced and whooped and told one another how brave they had been – and Gunnar felt fury growing inside him. "We'll get out of this," Mother whispered. "I'll think of a way to get us out of this."

She hugged him, but Gunnar barely noticed. He saw the people of the farm cowering in fear. Many were wailing at the sight of Father's body, and the Wolf Men snapped at them, like dogs snarling at sheep. Gunnar's fury grew hotter, fiercer, and he pushed Father's amulet deep into the pocket of his leggings.

"You know, Grim, I've a good mind to make this my home for a few years," Skuli said. "It's a better farm than any of my others, and it won't take long to rebuild the longhouse. Mind you, I'll need a wife to take care of it. What about it, Helga? Would you like to be a rich man's wife?"

Gunnar looked up. Skuli was standing over them, staring down at Mother, a cruel smile on his lips, Grim behind him, smirking. Mother stared back at Skuli defiantly, her face pale and smudged with ashes.

"I am the wife of Bjorn Sigurdsson," she said. "And such will I always be."

Skuli snorted and nodded at Father's body. "Well, he can't do you much good now, can he?" he said. "Marry me and you might be a queen some day."

"I'd rather be dead," said Mother, her eyes narrowed. She spat on Skuli's boots. "And I'll stick a knife in your ribs rather than let you touch me."

Grim moved forward, raising his hand to strike her, and she stared at him, her eyes full of hate. But Skuli grabbed Grim's arm.

"No, leave her, Grim," he said. "She's got a right to be angry with me. After all, I have just had her husband slaughtered, and seized her home."

"This steading will never be yours, Skuli!" yelled

Gunnar, unable to control himself. "It was my father's, and now it's mine!"

"Ah, the son speaks!" said Skuli. He grabbed Gunnar and yanked him to his feet. Mother screamed, but Grim held her down. "What are we going to do with the boy, Grim?" said Skuli. Grim shrugged. "Maybe I should adopt him. How would you like to be the son of a king, boy? That would make you a prince."

"Murderer!" yelled Gunnar, lashing out, trying to punch and kick him. "I hate you! I am Gunnar, son of Bjorn Sigurdsson, and I swear on the blood of my ancestors I will take vengeance on you for the murder of my father."

Skuli held him at arm's length and laughed, the man's iron grip biting into the flesh of Gunnar's shoulder. "You don't know what you're talking about, boy," said Skuli. "A blood oath isn't a thing to be taken lightly."

"I know that," hissed Gunnar, although he wasn't exactly sure what a blood oath involved. But saying it had certainly felt right.

"What a family you are!" said Skuli, shaking his

head once more. "I offer your father the chance of power and riches, and he says no thanks, he'd rather just be a farmer. I offer to make your mother a queen and you a prince, and you both threaten to kill me! Where's the gratitude? Here, Grim, you have him."

Skuli pushed Gunnar over to the other man. Grim threw a mail-clad arm round his throat and Gunnar almost choked, his nostrils filling with the smell of oiled steel and old sweat.

"What are you going to do?" said Mother.

"Well, that's an interesting question, Helga," said Skuli, smiling down at her again. "I was thinking of being nice to the lad, of making friends with him so you'd come round to the idea of marrying me. Then he went and spoiled things with that oath of his."

Gunnar tried to speak, but Grim squeezed tighter, silencing him.

"He can't hurt a man like you," Mother said. "He's just a boy."

"Little boys grow up to be big boys," said Skuli. "And I can't take the risk that he'll turn out to be as good a warrior as his father. Don't worry, Helga, you'll have plenty more sons, I can promise you that. Kill him, Grim."

"*NO!*" Mother screamed again, more horrified, more desperate than before. She flung herself at Grim, and two Wolf Men grabbed her and held her down, even though she flailed and kicked and tried to bite them.

Gunnar fought too, but Grim grabbed his hair and pushed him to his knees. He heard the sound of a dagger being pulled from its scabbard and struggled even harder as Grim yanked his head backwards. "Hold still, you little swine," Grim snarled. Suddenly the man's grip seemed to relax, and Gunnar saw Skuli looking up at the sky with a puzzled expression.

Something was coming in a blaze of light and a great beating of wings.

# FOUR
## NIGHTMARE
## CREATURES

ALL EYES WERE turned in the same direction, out over the sea. A huge ball of light had appeared on the horizon and was moving towards them, silver beams radiating from it across the white-capped waves, the pulse of beating wings growing louder the closer it came.

Grim had let go of Gunnar, and he rose to his feet just as the radiance broke into an arrowhead shape made up of nine separate lights. For a moment Gunnar thought it was a skein of magical, glowing geese, the brightest at the tip, the rest angled behind it, four on either side. Then he gasped, and there were screams from those around him as the shapes gradually became clear. The lights were enormous flying wolves with riders on their backs.

Gunnar glanced at Mother – and was amazed to see her smiling.

"I fear no man," muttered Skuli, eyes narrowed, hand on his sword hilt. "But what monsters are these? This must be a dream, or some kind of madness!"

"It's neither," said Mother, turning to glare at him. "Don't you recognize them from the old stories, you fool? Don't you know who they are?" Her voice rose until it almost cracked. "They're coming! *Odin's Valkyries are coming!*"

Gunnar knew about the Valkyries. They were Odin's

41

shield maidens, legendary beings who rode winged wolves. In the old tongue their name meant Choosers of the Fallen, and Odin sent them to collect the bravest men, any warrior who fought against great odds and was killed with a sword in his hand. The Valkyries carried them to Valhalla, the Hall of Fallen Heroes, where they would feast until the day of Ragnarok, the terrible reckoning at the end of time, when they would fight for Odin against the forces of darkness.

Now Gunnar understood why Mother was smiling. The Valkyries were coming for the only man who had died a true hero's death that night.

At last the beating of enormous wings filled the air above them and the giant wolves swept down to land. The flames in the longhouse had begun to subside, but now there was a greater brightness, the wolves and their riders giving off an eerie, shimmering glow that reached out to touch everything with silver, even the trees in the forest and the high snowy peaks of the distant mountains.

The wolves were creatures of nightmare, each the size of a horse, but with bristling grey pelts and

42

huge, leathery wings. Their eyes glowed red, and blood dripped from their muzzles as if they had come from some ghastly carrion feast, which might have explained the foul odour they brought with them. They swished their tails, snarling and showing their glistening fangs, swinging their massive heads from side to side, tugging at the reins held by their riders.

The Valkyries were an even more terrifying sight than the wolves. Gunnar felt a chill of fear as he studied them – nine tall women warriors in black chainmail and black cloaks, all holding red shields and spears with leaf-shaped blades, the points sparkling like stars. Their faces were completely hidden in black helmets with visors in the shape of a raven's curved beak.

There was muttering in the crowd, desperate prayers to Odin and Thor and the whimperings of those whose minds had given way. The four surviving dogs of the Wolf Men lay with stomachs pressed to the ground, ears flat to their heads, whining in terror. The leading Valkyrie dismounted and walked over to Father's body. She took off her helmet, and Gunnar gasped as her coldly beautiful face was revealed. Her long black hair had the glossy sheen of a raven's wing and her eyes were like two dark pools.

"I am Brunhild, Queen of the Valkyries," she said, her voice echoing in Gunnar's head. "Who speaks for this warrior? Who will tell me his name?"

For a long moment nobody dared reply, the only sounds the steady crackling of flames and the whining of the dogs. Gunnar stepped forward. Brunhild turned to face him, her eyes boring into his. But he stood his ground, meeting her eyes with his head held high, refusing to show he was scared.

"I speak for my father," he said. "I am Gunnar Bjornsson, and he is ... I mean, he *was*..." His voice faltered, and he felt tears fill his eyes, but he steadied himself and carried on, his voice gaining strength with every word. "He was Bjorn, son of Sigurd, holder of this steading that has been ours since before remembering. And that coward had him murdered!"

Gunnar spat out the last part and pointed an accusing finger at Skuli. Brunhild swung round to stare at the man. Grim and the rest of the Wolf Men

44

had backed away, their faces masks of terror. Skuli was left alone with Gunnar and Mother, Father's body beside them. But he met Brunhild's gaze too.

"It was battle, not murder," Skuli said, shrugging. "He gave as good as he got."

"But it was *you* who attacked *us*, *you* who killed Arnor and Ranulf and burned down our home," Gunnar yelled. "My father was only defending his family. He had no quarrel with you!"

"Such is the way of things, boy," snapped Skuli. "Man is wolf to man."

"But what you did was a crime!" said Gunnar, turning to Brunhild. "Aren't you going to punish him for it? Isn't that what the Gods are for?"

"We are servants of the Gods, not Gods ourselves," said Brunhild. "We take fallen warriors to Valhalla. You must pray to Odin for anything more."

Gunnar stared at her, desperately trying to think of something he could say that would make her help him. For the briefest of instants he thought he could see a softening in those cold, raven eyes, but he couldn't be sure.

"Come, Gunnar," said Mother. "We must let them take your father."

He looked at her, and she smiled and kissed his forehead. Gunnar gave in, and Mother and son stood next to each other, their hands clasped.

"Sisters! Lift up the fallen warrior!" said Brunhild. The Valkyries dismounted and lashed their spears together, covering them with their cloaks to make a bier. They raised Father from the ground and placed him on it, breaking off the arrow in his chest and laying Death-Bringer there, folding his fingers round the hilt. At last Brunhild and her Valkyries climbed into their saddles.

"Wait!" said Gunnar. He ran over to Brunhild and grabbed her reins, gazing up at her as she towered above him on her wolf. The creature growled softly and shook its huge head. "Skuli ordered Grim to kill me just before you came," Gunnar said quietly. "How can I save myself?"

Brunhild stared down at him. "This might be your day to die, or it might not. Only the Norns truly know what your fate will be in this world, Gunnar.

But now is the moment when you must say goodbye to your father."

Gunnar let go of her reins, a picture forming in his mind of three old women in ragged black cloaks – *the Norns*... Mother came across to him, and they bent to kiss Father. Brunhild spurred her mount into the air, the Valkyries following her, and they flew into the dark sky with a great beating of wings.

"That was incredible, amazing..." muttered Grim, shaking his head and staring at the glow on the horizon. He moved forward to stand beside Skuli. "I never thought I'd see anything like that and live to tell the tale."

"And just what kind of tale will that be, Grim?" said Skuli. "One about how brave you were? It had better not be. You and your lads behaved like a bunch of frightened girls. It was only me and the boy who stood up to them."

"So you don't want me to kill him?" said Grim, looking puzzled.

"Did I say that?" muttered Skuli. "The boy definitely takes after his father, which means I want

him dead more than ever. Get on with it, Grim."

"Yes, of course," spluttered Grim. "You men, hold the boy!"

Gunnar went cold as the nearest two Wolf Men moved towards him. Then he sighed. What was the point of struggling? Maybe it was better to give up, to end all this anguish. Grim was advancing, dagger in hand, and Gunnar could almost feel the steel blade slicing into his throat already.

Then Mother grabbed a knife from the belt of the nearest Wolf Man and slashed at Grim with it, an arc of blood spraying from his cheek. Skuli and the other Wolf Men stared at Mother with their mouths open.

"*RUN!*" she screamed at Gunnar, their eyes locking for an instant, and he knew she was giving him what might be his only chance to live.

So he fled. He dodged the grasping hands of a Wolf Man, who slipped and fell behind him. He ran past the people of the farm, hurdled the still-terrified, whining dogs, and headed for the gate and the forest beyond.

He heard Skuli yelling and realized he was being

chased. An arrow whistled past his cheek. He ducked to one side, and a second arrow just missed him. A third hit the gatepost as he ran through the open gate. But now his feet were on the track into the forest, the trees ahead of him like a solid wall of darkness, the cold wind rustling through their tops and making a noise like the sea.

Ten paces to go, five paces ... and he was swallowed up, the outside world gone, the shadows between the trunks as black as death.

# FIVE
## AT THE GOD
## HOUSE

GUNNAR KEPT RUNNING as long as he dared. At last he slowed down and stepped off the track, groping through the undergrowth until he came to what felt like a huge oak. He curled up between its roots, hugged himself and sobbed.

After a while he pulled himself together, wiping his eyes and nose on the sleeve of his tunic. He listened for the sounds of a search, but all he could hear was the wind still sighing in the tree-tops. He guessed they would come after him as soon as the sun rose, and that didn't leave him much time to work out a plan. Where could he go? What was he going to *do*?

It was hard to think clearly with a mind so full of grief for Father – and hatred for Skuli. Gunnar had never hated anyone before, but now he savoured the feeling, letting its heat flood through his veins. He had sworn an oath of vengeance against Skuli, and he was determined to fulfil it, even if he had to go to the ends of the Earth and back to do so…

That thought hit Gunnar like a blow to the face. No, he wouldn't go to the ends of the Earth – *he would travel to Valhalla instead and fetch Father back!* As Mother had said, he was just a boy, so how could he take revenge on Skuli? A man like that would eat him alive. But he could fulfil his oath by freeing Father, who could then kill Skuli and save Mother. Odin must bring the fallen heroes back to life somehow – otherwise how could they fight for him?

But he had no flying wolf to take him to Valhalla. He didn't even know where it was, or if it was possible to get there by some other means – none of the old stories went into that kind of detail. Then he remembered what Brunhild had said – *you must pray to Odin for anything more*. Well, if anyone knew where Valhalla was it should be Odin, the God who had created it.

Gunnar looked up. The sky was beginning to lighten, a pale glow seeping into the darkness. He thought quickly; he could pray to Odin here in the forest of course, but there was a better place, somewhere he had been for the midwinter ceremony at Yuletide, for the blood sacrifices before the spring planting, for the harvest festival – the temple they called the God House.

He rose to his feet, found the track once more, and headed into the gloom. By the time the sun had risen fully he was out of the forest and on the track towards the mountains. After a while he came to the top of a ridge and walked down into a valley. The track took him through a grove of ancient oak trees, scraps of morning mist clinging to their branches, and then into a broad clearing.

He shivered at the sight of the wooden building in front of him. The God House had always made him nervous. It looked like a dragon, its walls painted to resemble scales, its entrance a mouth with fangs carved into the curved doorposts, a pair of yellow eyes above. And to complete the picture, leading up to the door was a red flagstone path like a fiery tongue.

Suddenly Gunnar heard squawking and he glanced up. Two crows were staring at him from the roof, heads tipped to one side – the sheen of their black feathers reminded him of Brunhild. They squawked again, and flapped their wings and hopped about, making Gunnar feel even more uneasy. He frowned at them, took a deep breath … then stepped over the temple's threshold.

The wooden floor was smooth, polished by the feet of those who came to worship there. Huge uprights – each one the trunk of an enormous tree – held up the roof beams, and every surface was carved with pictures of Gods and giants, elves and dwarves, men and strange beasts, scenes from all the old stories. An altar stood at the far end, a flat-topped rock stained with the blood of sacrifices. In his mind Gunnar could see the bleating lamb, the knife flashing and the blood pulsing out, while the people of his steading looked on and chanted prayers.

Now some of those people were dead and the future for the rest was bleak, unless he could do something about it. A prayer on its own might not be enough, not without an offering of some kind, and Gunnar had no lamb or goat to sacrifice on the altar. Other kinds of offering were sometimes made, things that were important to someone or had a value, however small. From his pocket, Gunnar pulled the only thing he had brought with him – Father's amulet.

It was a simple image of Thor's hammer carved in black stone, his last link with Father and home, with the life Skuli had stolen. He laid it on the altar.

"Hear me, great Odin," he said softly. "I beg for your help in the task that lies before me. But most of all I ask you this – how can I get to Valhalla?"

"Well, the usual way is to die in battle with a sword in your hand," said a quiet, deep voice behind him. "But you look a little young for that."

Gunnar turned round. An old man stood in the doorway. He was tall, his face powerful and striking. His beard was white, and he wore the clothes of a traveller – a hat with a wide brim that dipped over one eye, a black cloak and tunic, thick trousers and strong boots. He had a bag slung over one shoulder, and he carried a wooden staff.

"You look tired and hungry too," the old man said. "I'd be happy to share with you the food I have."

For an instant Gunnar wondered if he should run. But the old man seemed friendly enough, and the mention of food had made the juices flow in his mouth. He needed to eat and he needed to rest. So he shrugged, and the old man walked out of the God House, beckoning him to follow.

A low byre stood near by. Gunnar recognized it as the place where beasts were kept tethered before they were sacrificed. The old man ducked inside and set about making a fire with straw and twigs he found in one of the stalls. Soon they were sitting, the fire crackling. The old man pulled cheese and a loaf from his bag and cut chunks with a small bone-handled knife. Gunnar tore into the food, not realizing how hungry he was until his stomach started to fill.

The old man had taken off his hat and Gunnar saw that the eye hidden by its brim till then was sightless, a milky-white ball like a shiny pebble. The other eye was the palest blue.

"So, what brings you to the God House this early?" said the old man after a while. "You look as if you've had an interesting night."

Gunnar glanced down at himself. He was filthy, his clothes and hands stained with ashes and dried blood. Father's blood. Hot tears filled his eyes and he tried to hold them in. What was he doing sitting here with this old man?

"Thanks for the food," he said, and rose to his feet. "But I have to leave."

"What's your hurry?" said the old man, throwing more twigs on the fire. "I might be able to help you get to Valhalla, if you really must go there."

Gunnar stared at him. There was something strange about this old man, something that made Gunnar feel uneasy, although he couldn't say why. He sat down once more and crossed his arms. "I'm listening," he said.

The old man smiled and cut off more bread and cheese, handing the chunks to Gunnar. "You've heard the stories, so you know Valhalla is to be found in Asgard, home of the Gods," he said. "You'll also know that Asgard is one of the nine worlds, and that all nine are linked by the great tree Yggdrasil. But Asgard itself is joined to this world by the rainbow bridge, Bifrost."

"I've heard of that," said Gunnar. "How do I find it?"

"Ah, well, that might not be so easy." The yellow flames of the fire were reflected in the old man's solitary eye. "Some say one end of Bifrost stands in the Land of Ice and Fire, a whole month's journey across the sea. And then of course you'll have to deal with Heimdall, guardian of the bridge."

"A whole *month*?" Gunnar's heart sank. It hadn't

occurred to him that getting to Valhalla would take so long. He tried not to think of what might happen to Mother and the steading in the meantime. But he had no choice – he would have to follow his plan. "Where can I find a ship that will take me?"

"There are usually plenty of ships in the harbour at Kaupang."

Gunnar had heard that name too, and had an idea it was a big town, but he knew nothing else about the place. "How do I get there? Is it far?"

"Three days by foot. Maybe more if the weather is bad."

Gunnar groaned, but then he found himself yawning. His eyelids seemed to be growing heavy, and his limbs too. He looked at the old man through the skeins of smoke from the fire and saw that he was smiling again.

"Who *are* you?" Gunnar asked. "I don't even know … your … name…"

"Oh, you'll know it one day, Gunnar, when you fly with the eagle to the Land of Ice and Fire," said the old man. It seemed as if his voice was coming from a great distance. "Sleep now; you must sleep…"

Gunnar lay down, his cheek cushioned on his hands. How did the old man know his name? He was sure he hadn't told him. Gunnar had a feeling the answer might be important, although he couldn't think why. Then a dark wave swept through his mind, filling it with blackness, and he knew no more.

He woke with a start and thought for a moment he was at home, until he sat up and remembered. It was almost dark outside the hut, a white mist creeping across the ground. Gunnar saw that the fire had gone out and he shivered. The old man had vanished, but he had left his bag, and Gunnar opened it. He found more bread and cheese, a flask of ale, a flint and a few silver coins.

And right at the bottom was a long grey feather from an eagle's wing.

# SIX
## THE RIGHT
# ROAD

HE SOON GOT the fire going again with the flint and ate some more bread and cheese, washing it down with the ale in the flask. Then he sat and brooded, staring sometimes at the yellow flames, sometimes at the feather.

The old man had been friendly and

generous – Gunnar guessed he had left the bag for him. But it had been a strange encounter. The old man had known his name without being told it, and hadn't been surprised to hear Gunnar talking about Valhalla. And what did he mean about *flying with the eagle to the Land of Ice and Fire*? Falling asleep like that had been odd too. Perhaps the old man was a sorcerer and had cast a spell on him...

Now Gunnar tutted, angry with himself. It had been natural for him to fall asleep, and perhaps he had told the old man his name and then forgotten. And maybe meeting Brunhild was making him think everything was strange. The old man had come and gone, and Gunnar felt he should just be grateful for his help. But he thought he'd better keep the feather safe, and tucked it in his pocket.

It was fully dark outside the byre now, and Gunnar knew there was no point in setting off for Kaupang before morning. He kept the fire going as long as he could, then tried to rest. He slept uneasily, his dreams filled with blood and fire, and woke feeling unrefreshed, his back aching, the cold deep in his bones.

He finished the bread and cheese and left the byre, the old man's bag on his shoulder. It was a crisp autumn day, the sun bright in a blue sky. The track that had brought Gunnar to the God House carried on, and he decided to follow it, hoping he would find someone who could tell him how to find Kaupang.

The track skirted the mountains and took him through low, rocky hills. Towards evening a shepherd told him he was already on the road for Kaupang. He passed the night in a cave, using the flint to make a fire, his stomach grumbling with hunger. On the second day the weather grew colder, the wind full of snow. Gunnar came to a village where he used one of the old man's coins to buy oatcakes and goat's cheese from an old woman, who offered him a bed for the night in her cow byre. And on the third day the track brought him to the crest of a ridge from which he looked down on Kaupang. He had arrived.

There were hundreds of huts, the smoke of cooking fires rising to hang in a blue-grey haze over their thatched roofs. Narrow alleys wriggled between the dwellings. Several bigger buildings stood among the huts, one in particular larger than the rest, perhaps the hall of some rich lord. Beyond it was the harbour, broad wharves with dozens of vessels tied up to them – lean longships with their proud dragon's head prows, fat cargo ships, a host of smaller boats nestling cosily between the others like piglets suckling from their mothers.

Gunnar walked on and entered the town. The alleys were crowded, and everyone seemed to be yelling at the tops of their voices. Some spoke the Norse tongue, although many had strange accents, and there were plenty whose speech Gunnar couldn't understand. Most of those looked wild and exotic – men with tattoos swirling over their faces, warriors in pointed helmets, women covered in jewels. There were ragged beggars everywhere, crying out for alms.

"Terrible, isn't it?" said a voice behind him. "It's the smell I can't stand."

Gunnar turned round. A boy a little older than him was standing near by, thumbs hooked in his belt, a grin on his face. He was wearing ordinary clothes and boots like Gunnar's and had a shock of fair hair and blue eyes. The boy's grin was open and friendly and Gunnar couldn't help smiling back.

"Mind you, the whole town stinks, not just the beggars," said the boy. "I hate to think what's in the mud of these alleys. My name's Gauk, by the way."

"I'm Gunnar ... Gunnar Bjornsson."

"Well then, Gunnar, son of Bjorn, what brings you to crowded, stinking old Kaupang? Nobody comes here without a good reason."

Gunnar paused. It would probably be a bad idea to tell the story of what had happened to him. If he started talking about Valkyries and Valhalla this boy might think he was mad, and a friend with local knowledge might prove useful.

"I've come to take passage on a ship," said Gunnar at last, deciding to tell Gauk the truth, although not all of it. "I have to find my father."

"Well, you won't be the last to go on *that* particular quest." Gauk put his arm round Gunnar's shoulders. "This is your lucky day. I know plenty of men who own ships, so there's nobody better to help you. But first things first. Let me treat you to breakfast. You look as if you could do with a good meal."

"You don't have to do that." Gunnar felt his cheeks flush. He didn't want Gauk to think he was poor like the beggars. "I can pay my own way."

"Of course you can, no offence meant!" said Gauk. He took Gunnar by the elbow and led him towards the entrance of a narrow alley. "I was just trying to be friendly – I know the best places to eat. There's a great tavern down here…"

Gunnar resisted, a small voice in the back of his mind warning him to be careful. But he was hungry, so he let Gauk pull him into an alley.

It was fine at first – but then gradually the huts seemed to close in on them. Strange faces peered at them from the shadows. A mangy dog growled from a door, a rat scuttled over Gunnar's foot, the mud grew thicker and smellier.

"Wait," Gunnar said. "Are you sure this is all right?"

Gauk smiled. "Nearly there," he said.

They soon came to a place where another,

narrower alley cut across the one they had been following. Gauk stopped and turned to face him.

"Is this it?" said Gunnar. He looked round, puzzled. The alleys were empty, the huts shuttered and silent. "I don't see any tavern here."

Suddenly two boys stepped out of the shadows. They were dirty and mean-looking and bigger than Gauk – and Gunnar. One was holding a wooden club the length of a man's forearm, and they were both smirking.

Gunnar took a step backward. The boy with the club stepped forward, and the other new arrival moved to cut off Gunnar's retreat.

"What's this all about?" said Gunnar. "I'm not looking for trouble."

"It seems you've found it anyway," said Gauk, still smiling. "My friends are called Ivar and Njal. Now hand me that bag of yours."

"No, I won't," said Gunnar.

Gauk shrugged, and Njal smashed his club into Gunnar's elbow. Gunnar cried out and dropped the bag, as pain shot from his shoulder to his fingertips.

Ivar picked up the bag and turned it upside down, tipping a few coins into the mud.

"That's not going to make us rich, is it?" said Gauk. "You're turning out to be a real disappointment, Gunnar. But at least we've got another way of making a profit from you. Well, don't just stand there, you two – tie him up!"

Njal and Ivar wrenched his arms behind his back. Gunnar cried out again, but Ivar silenced him with a punch to the gut, and he felt them tying his wrists together, the rough twine biting into his flesh. Then they hustled him away down one of the dark alleys, Gauk following behind.

"Where are you taking me?" said Gunnar at last, struggling to catch his breath. He was stumbling and splashing through the stinking mud, Ivar and Njal each holding one of his arms, and his elbow felt as if it was on fire.

"Why, to meet the king, of course!" said Gauk, laughing. "Lead on, lads!"

# SEVEN
## THE KING
## OF KAUPANG

A FEW MOMENTS later they arrived at the doors of the hall Gunnar had seen from the ridge, the one he'd guessed belonged to a rich lord. He was dragged through the porch past racks of spears and into the dark interior. He caught a glimpse of long tables and benches and faces, and then he was flung down on the reed-covered floor.

A fire burned in the hearth, big logs crackling and spitting. Beyond it a huge man sat on a throne of bones, a pair of giant narwhal tusks crossing above his head. He was bald and fat, the flesh of his jowls merging into his neck as if they had melted, the mountain of his body covered in a fine red tunic. He wore a thick gold chain round his neck and gold rings on all his fingers, and he stared at Gunnar, his eyes like those of a lizard, cold and unblinking.

"What's this you've brought me, Gauk?" the man said, his voice so deep it seemed to come from somewhere in his vast belly. "A gift? You shouldn't have. But then you're such a generous, good-hearted lad."

The rest of the hall had fallen silent, and Gunnar sensed people gathering in the shadows around him to watch what was going on. Half a dozen hard-faced warriors stood behind the throne, hands on their sword hilts.

"A new boy for your slave pens, Orm," said

Gauk. "I only wish I could make you a gift of him, but alas…"

"What did you say?" hissed Gunnar, glaring at Gauk and trying to get to his feet. "I'm freeborn. You can't sell me like some farm animal!"

"We can do whatever we want with you!" hissed Ivar, cuffing him round the head.

Njal grabbed the back of Gunnar's neck and pushed him down, grinding his face into the floor. "Now … just … keep … quiet," he said. Gunnar struggled, but his mouth was full of dirt and reeds, and Njal's hands were strong.

"My heart bleeds for you," said Orm, studying Gauk with narrowed eyes. "But I'm not in the market for any more slaves just now. My pens are full."

"I don't believe it," said Gauk. "You're always interested in a bargain. I'm not even going to ask you for the going rate. Just give me five gold pieces."

"Show me his face again," rumbled Orm. Gunnar gasped as Ivar grabbed his hair and pulled his head up. It felt as if his scalp was being ripped off his skull. "He looks better than the filthy scrapings of the alleys you usually bring me," said Orm. "But I'd still be mad to pay you more than two gold pieces."

"Now it's my heart that's bleeding," said Gauk. "I'll settle for four."

"Three, and that's my final offer. Take it or leave it."

"Done. You're a hard man, Orm, but a fair one."

Orm snorted like a walrus. "Pay him, Rurik," he said.

Njal let go of Gunnar. One of the men behind Orm stepped forward and counted coins into Gauk's hand. "So long, Gunnar," said Gauk. "We wish you happiness in your new home – wherever that may be, of course."

They strolled away, and the others in the hall drifted back to whatever they had been doing. "Put our new purchase in the pens, Rurik," said Orm.

"You're not putting me in any slave pen!" Gunnar yelled. "I'm no thrall!"

"Oh, but you are, boy," growled Orm. He smiled, his white teeth glinting in the firelight. "You've been bought and paid for."

Gunnar started to protest again, but Rurik pulled him to his feet. The big man had hair the colour of straw, but his beard was brown, and his eyes were greeny-grey, reminding Gunnar strangely of Mother's. "Give it up, or Orm will make me beat you," said Rurik. "That's something neither you nor I will enjoy."

There was gentleness in the big man's voice, and sense in what he'd said too. So Gunnar did as he was told, and let himself be led out of the hall. He needed to think, to work out what to do. But then they entered a courtyard, and Gunnar saw something that soon had him dragging his feet, a line of enclosures made of wooden stakes lashed together – like animal pens, but for people instead.

Those packed into the pens were young and old, tall and short, fair- or dark-skinned, but all of them were quiet, expressions of despair or blankness on their faces. Somehow the silence made it worse. Gunnar felt his soul start to shrivel, and wondered how long it would be before he looked the same.

Rurik dragged him across the courtyard, past some

guards standing round a brazier, its flames flapping in the cold wind. Gunnar expected to be put straight in the pens, but Rurik led him towards a smithy in the far corner.

Rurik pushed Gunnar inside and then stooped to follow him through the wide entrance; the stifling heat hit Gunnar like a blow. A dark, sour-faced man was standing at a big anvil. He wore a leather apron and was banging away with a heavy hammer at a rod of white-hot metal, his huge arms and shoulders shining with sweat, the forge behind him glowing red like the mouth of a dragon. Pieces of metal of all sizes and more tools – tongs, pokers, a shovel – leaned against the walls.

"You know what to do, Hogni, you miserable wretch," growled Rurik. "And hurry up. I don't want to be near you for any longer than I have to."

"The feeling is mutual, you backstabber," growled the smith. He held up the metal with a pair of tongs, and Gunnar saw it was shaped into a ring that wasn't quite closed. "So it's lucky for you this one is nearly ready."

There was hatred in the exchange, but for all Gunnar cared they could kill each other on the spot – and Orm and everybody else who worked for him. All he wanted to think about was escape. He was sure he could outrun Rurik and the guards, although he wouldn't get far with his hands tied. He strained against the binding, but sensed that he was being studied. Rurik was staring at him.

"Nothing to say, boy? At this point new slaves are usually weeping for their mothers and begging to be set free. You just seem to be thinking."

"I've got plenty to think about," said Gunnar. "What will happen to me?"

"The pig Hogni here will fit you with a nice, shiny thrall ring to go round your neck," said Rurik. "Then Orm will put you up for sale. He buys and sells slaves, and he's the richest man in town, which is why he's called the King of Kaupang even though he doesn't have a drop of royal blood in that fat body of his. After you've been sold you'd better just hope for a kindly master."

The smith dipped the thrall ring into a bucket of

water. There was a great hissing noise and clouds of white steam. He took it out again and approached Gunnar, pulling it open so he could slip it round the boy's neck.

Gunnar had a feeling this was probably his last chance. "When are you going to untie my wrists?" he asked Rurik. "I can't feel my hands any more."

Rurik smiled and shrugged. "We can't have that now, can we?" he said. He unsheathed the dagger on his belt and cut through the bindings.

As soon as Gunnar's hands were free he stepped over to the wall and grabbed the shovel. He swung it round by the shaft and smashed the flat of the wide blade into the smith's face. There was a dull *clang* and the crunching noise of bone breaking, and Hogni staggered back, toppling over the anvil, crashing down behind it in a terrific clattering of tools and thrall rings. Gunnar threw the shovel aside and dashed out of the smithy, listening for the clamour of pursuit.

But all he could hear was the sound of Rurik roaring with laughter.

# EIGHT
## A SILVER
## ARM RING

THE GUARDS CAUGHT him before he'd run ten paces. Gunnar struggled and kicked and cursed, but they pinned him down in the foul mud of the courtyard. "Hey, Rurik, what do you want us to do with him?" yelled the older guard.

"*Do* with him, Thorkel?" Rurik said, walking over to them. "Why, slap him on the back and tell him what a good lad he is! That boy has just given me the biggest laugh I've had in years. *Clang!* And Hogni went flying."

"What in Odin's name are you talking about, Rurik?" Thorkel said, frowning. He had piercing blue eyes, grey hair tied in a ponytail, and wore a thick brown tunic. A decent-looking sword in a wooden scabbard rode on his hip.

"The boy smashed Hogni's face with a shovel," said Rurik. "Maybe it's made him look better. It couldn't have made him any uglier, could it?"

Thorkel smiled at him and shook his head. "I'm not sure Hogni agrees," he said, nodding at the smithy. Gunnar strained to look round. The smith was striding towards them, blood running from his nose.

"I'll kill him, I swear," Hogni growled. "I'll strangle the little swine!"

There was a sudden hiss of steel. Hogni stopped instantly and fell silent. The point of Rurik's sword was resting on the soft white skin of his throat.

"Orm wouldn't be very happy with me if I allowed you to kill a slave before he had a chance to make a profit on him," Rurik said quietly. "So on your way, Hogni, or I'll let the boy have another go at you."

The guards sniggered, and Hogni scowled. "One day, Rurik, I'm going to cut your heart out and eat it," he snarled, and stomped back to his smithy.

"So then, Rurik," said Thorkel. "Is the boy for the pens, or what?"

"No, I don't think so." Rurik rubbed his chin and stared after Hogni thoughtfully. "Come on, boy, we're going to see Orm again."

Rurik pulled a confused Gunnar to his feet and marched him into the hall once more. Orm stared coldly from his seat at the warrior and the boy.

"It's your lucky day, Orm," said Rurik. "I've decided I need a slave, so you won't have to go to the trouble of putting this one on the auction block."

Gunnar turned to look at him, wondering what could be going through the big man's mind. He had expected Rurik to tell Orm what had just happened, and for Orm to order a beating for him. Or something worse.

"Is that so?" said Orm. He seemed surprised too. "What's brought this on? I've never known you buy a slave before. I doubt you can pay my price."

"I can," said Rurik. "This should be enough."

Rurik took a thick silver arm ring from under one sleeve of his byrnie. He tossed it to Orm, and the fat man caught it. He raised his gaze to Rurik and smiled. "You're right, this will do nicely," he said. "The boy is yours."

Rurik nodded and pushed Gunnar out of the hall. Then he strode off down a nearby alley, keeping the boy moving ahead. Soon they came to a hut and went inside. A ring of hearth stones stood in the middle, a fur-covered bracken bed against one wall, a wooden chest against the other.

"Don't be worried, boy," said Rurik. He eased his sword belt over his head and tossed it on the bed. Then he kneeled by the hearth and poked at the ashes with a bit of kindling. "I'm not going to eat you. Make yourself at home."

81

"This is not my home," said Gunnar. "And I will never be your slave."

For a moment Gunnar thought Rurik hadn't heard. The big man blew onto the ashes in the hearth and a red glow appeared that he fed with more kindling. "What's your name?" Rurik said eventually. "At least tell me that."

"Gunnar." Yellow flames were starting to flicker over the wood.

"Just Gunnar?" Rurik sat with his back against the chest and crossed his legs. "Suit yourself. And I don't suppose you're going to tell me how you ended up being sold as a slave by Gauk of the Silver Tongue, are you?"

Gunnar shrugged. "There's nothing to tell."

"There's always a story to tell, and I can probably guess some of yours. Your clothes are of fine quality, but they're stained with blood. So you're of good family, but something bad must have happened. Am I right?"

"Maybe," said Gunnar.

"You're a tough one, I'll give you that." Rurik

grinned. "And you're a fighter. That's what I like about you."

"So let me go," Gunnar said quickly. "I swear I'll find the money to pay you back. But I can't be your slave. I can't stay here."

Rurik's grin vanished. "Listen, boy. Until today you might have thought you were free, but this was always going to be your fate, foretold by the Norns."

That same image of three ancient women in ragged black clothes filled Gunnar's mind again. He remembered Brunhild talking of them too, and he suddenly felt angry. "What have they got to do with me? I've heard them mentioned in old stories, but I don't even know who they are."

"They know you," said Rurik. "Some call them the Norns, others the Three Sisters. They sit at the foot of the great tree Yggdrasil and weave a web in which each thread is a life – its past, present and future. They decide all that will happen from the day we're born to the day they cut our threads – and we die."

Gunnar wondered if it was true. Had he always been doomed to see his home burned and Father murdered, and to end up a slave? If so, there was no point fighting against it, and he might as well give up any idea of bringing Father back from Valhalla and saving Mother. But a new thought occurred to him and he spoke it out loud before he could catch himself. "What if this isn't my *final* fate? What if my fate will lead me to other things?"

"Perhaps it will," said Rurik. "*My* fate has brought me to this stinking hole. You might find your way to somewhere else, but for now you're my slave, and you'd better get used to the idea. As fates go, it's not that bad."

"Really?" Gunnar scowled at him. "How did you work that out?"

"I'll be a kindly master. I won't beat you or make you work too hard."

"But you've never bought a slave before. Why did you buy *me*?"

"I thought it would be worth it just to see Hogni's face when he finds out I've bought you, and that you're going to be around all the time…"

Gunnar's heart sank – he was to be Rurik's means of

tormenting the smith. His presence in Kaupang would be a constant reminder to everyone that Hogni's nose had been flattened by a mere slave boy. So not only was he stuck here when he should be on his way to Valhalla, he was caught in a feud between two violent men. "Why do you hate each other?" he asked.

"I played a prank on Hogni one evening when I was bored, and he didn't like it," sighed Rurik. "Harsh words were spoken, threats were made."

Gunnar frowned, hardly able to believe that was all there was to it. "And what if I still say no to being a slave?" he said, looking Rurik in the eye. "What if I refuse to accept it's my fate, and try to escape again the first chance I get?"

"So you're stubborn too. Well then, I'd better show you."

Rurik picked up his sword belt and put it on again, then ducked out through the hut's door, beckoning Gunnar to follow. The sky was darkening over the town, the air growing colder. Rurik's stride was long and his left hand rested easily on his sword hilt, and most people quickly got out of his way.

"This will do," said Rurik at last. "We can see them from here."

They had arrived on the quayside. The tide had ebbed and many of the ships were tilted onto their sides, the setting sun casting deep shadows. Gulls swooped and squawked, and a mud-and-sea smell filled Gunnar's nostrils. But there was another odour too, something foul and disturbing.

"See what?" he asked, looking round at Rurik. The big man said nothing. He nodded at a couple of posts stuck in the mud twenty paces from the quayside, a pair of roughly trimmed logs the height of a man.

Now Gunnar understood where the stench was coming from. A dead body was tied to each post, the flesh puffy and green, white bones poking through sodden rags that had once been clothes.

"That's what happens to slaves who try to escape," said Rurik. "They soon get caught – the locals and most of the ship crews know it doesn't pay to make an enemy of Orm. Once they're returned, he has them tied to the posts at low tide and lets the sea kill them. It's not a good death, or a quick one."

Gunnar stared at the posts, then lifted his gaze to the open sea. The Land of Ice and Fire was somewhere across those waves...

# NINE
## FRIENDS
## AND ENEMIES

THERE WAS STILL the matter of Gunnar's thrall ring to be settled. Orm heard about what had happened and sent another of his men to Rurik's hut with a message. Gunnar was to have a ring fitted by Hogni, and that was the end of it.

"Come on, boy," said Rurik. "You'll have to swallow your pride."

Night had fallen by the time they entered the courtyard again, the smithy's forge casting the only light. The guards crowded round the front of the smithy, laughing and nudging one another, clearly hoping for more entertainment. Rurik pushed through, pulling Gunnar along behind him. Hogni looked up from his anvil, and Gunnar saw that his face was bruised and swollen.

"You've got some gall coming in here, Rurik," he growled, glaring at them. "Unless you've brought the boy back so I can kill him after all."

"No, Hogni, that's not what's going to happen," Rurik answered. "We're here because Orm says the boy must have a thrall ring like the other slaves. And as he belongs to me now, just make sure you don't do him any harm."

"What are you talking about?" muttered Hogni, looking confused.

"I bought the boy from Orm," said Rurik with a grin. "Cost me a silver arm ring. But it was worth it just to know he'll be protecting me from you."

The guards howled with laughter. Suddenly two more men barged into the smithy past Thorkel and the rest and went over to stand by Hogni. One was a young man with a cruel mouth, the other a balding warrior who was missing most of his right ear. Both wore chainmail byrnies, the young man's particularly fine, although Gunnar noticed that his stomach bulged over his sword belt.

"Well now, this *is* an honour," said Rurik. "A visit from Prince Starkad the Stupid and ugly old Ari One-Ear. What can we do for you?"

The one-eared warrior grabbed his sword hilt, but Starkad put a hand on his arm. "Let's not have any trouble, Ari," he said, smiling. Starkad reminded Gunnar of somebody, but he couldn't think who. "Rurik likes to tease," Starkad went on. "Mind you, that will probably be the death of him some day."

"You think so?" said Rurik. He gripped his own sword hilt. "We'll see which one of us comes to a sticky end first." He turned to Thorkel and the other guards. "What do you reckon, lads? Will it be me or Starkad?"

"Don't do anything you'll regret, Rurik," muttered Thorkel.

Rurik slowly took his hand off his hilt. "The only thing I regret is that I might have missed supper in the hall. So if you could get Hogni to do what Orm wants, Starkad, my new slave and I will be on our way. It's strange, though, I've never understood why you and our idiot smith should be friends."

"It's really no surprise, Rurik," Starkad said smoothly, smiling again. "A common enemy can often bring men together. Hogni, do as Rurik says."

Hogni glared, his face dark with anger. But soon Gunnar was kneeling while the smith welded the thrall ring shut with the red-hot tip of a poker, the bitter reek of worked iron filling his nostrils. He half expected the smith to burn him with the poker, but Rurik made sure Hogni knew he was watching closely.

Gunnar rose to his feet at last, the ring heavy round his neck. Rurik walked out, pushing past Thorkel and his men. Starkad, Ari and Hogni watched him go, and Gunnar hurried after him across the courtyard and into the hall.

"Who is Starkad, Rurik?" he said. "Why did you call him Prince?"

"What else would you have me call the King of Kaupang's son and heir?" said Rurik. "Some day all this will be his, and he's welcome to it."

Rurik took a seat at a table, and Gunnar stood behind him. He could see the resemblance between Orm and his son now. Starkad didn't yet have his father's bulk, but they had the same sinister smile. Was Starkad his enemy now too, along with Hogni? Gunnar told himself he didn't care. The only thing that mattered was getting out of Kaupang and bringing Father back from Valhalla. He wasn't going to be frightened by feuds or the sight of a few rotting corpses in the harbour. He'd just have to be clever, keep his eyes open, find a way.

The days passed, the north wind brought snow, and Gunnar learned to be a slave. He lived in Rurik's hut and slept by the hearth like a dog, although Rurik kept his word and was a kindly master. There was plenty for Gunnar to do – errands to run, weapons and armour to clean – but Gunnar soon came to believe Rurik was uncomfortable with the idea of owning a slave. The only time he seemed to like it was when he could flaunt Gunnar in front of Hogni.

Before long Gunnar felt he knew Kaupang as well as the Great Fjord. The town was always full of people – Vikings from the northern lands, tall, fair-haired Saxons from England, Irishmen with intricately tattooed faces and bodies. There were loud, bearded Franks from further south, wild-eyed Huns from the lands of the Rus beyond the Baltic, even dark-skinned Moors.

There were traders as well, quick-tongued men who came to buy and sell whatever would bring a profit. And there were the slaves – men, women and children from everywhere. Gunnar was one of them now, and got his fair share of kicks and curses. Although no one dared mistreat him when Rurik was around.

Gunnar also came to know more about Orm and the people of his hall. Orm had twenty or so warriors – Orm's Hounds, as they were known. He had a wife too, a scrawny, red-haired, bad-tempered woman called Vigdis who was always yelling at servants and slaves, when she wasn't beating them, that is.

But Rurik remained a mystery. Gunnar felt he should understand his master, so one day, on the way back from an errand, he decided to ask Thorkel about him. Thorkel had taken a liking to Gunnar and was always happy to talk.

"Rurik? He's a mystery to me too," said Thorkel with a smile. Gunnar had found him alone in the courtyard, wrapped in an old sheepskin, standing close to the brazier and stamping his feet on the snow. "He walked into the hall one night two summers ago and asked Orm if he needed another warrior. Orm made him fight Ari as a test, and that's how Ari lost his ear. He's lucky Rurik didn't cut him to pieces. Orm's no fool, and he could see Rurik was the real thing."

"What do you mean? Aren't they all warriors?"

"Appearances can deceive, Gunnar." Thorkel's smile faded. "Plenty of men think they can be warriors. But there's a world of difference between

94

pushing women and children and slaves around and being a man your shield brothers can depend on when the sky darkens with arrows and blades rise and fall. I've seen all that. I haven't always spent my days guarding Orm's slave pens. I can tell you, Rurik is as good a warrior as you'll find."

"Is that why Starkad hates him? He makes no secret of it."

"Starkad is full of envy," said Thorkel. "He wishes he could be a warrior like Rurik. So he plots against Rurik, and tries to make the other men hate him too."

"But what about Orm? He likes Rurik, doesn't he?"

"Orm does what's best for Orm. It suits him to have Rurik around, so he lets him get away with a lot. You would have lost an eye or a hand for what you did to Hogni if Rurik hadn't bought you. But Rurik is his own worst enemy, especially when he's bored or has one of his dark moods."

Gunnar knew what Thorkel meant. Every so often a black cloud of gloom seemed to settle on Rurik. He would fall silent for a day, as if speaking were too painful, and he would lie on his bed, or go to a tavern and get drunk.

"Why does he have them? Did something happen to him, Thorkel?"

"Ah, that I don't know." A blast of wind made the flames flap in the brazier, and Thorkel shivered and pulled his sheepskin more tightly round him. "But I can guess. He was once a warrior in the Greek Emperor's guard, and now he serves a fat slave-trader in filthy Kaupang. It's not Miklagard, is it?"

Just then Gunnar heard a harsh chattering noise behind him and looked round. Two magpies were standing on the roof of Hogni's smithy, flapping their wings up and down and staring at him. "Did you say … the Greek Emperor's guard?" he murmured, slowly turning back to Thorkel. "In Miklagard?"

"I did," Thorkel answered, his eyes narrowed. "Is it important?"

"No," said Gunnar. But it was very important indeed.

# TEN
## SHADOW OF
## THE PAST

GUNNAR HEADED BACK to Rurik's hut deep in thought. Father had been a warrior in the Greek Emperor's guard too, so he and Rurik might have known each other, perhaps

a few gold coins, trapping him in Kaupang when he should have been on his quest. Njal was on all fours groping for his club in the mud. Gunnar stamped on his hand, grinding into it with his heel and feeling the knuckle-bones crack. Njal howled, and Gunnar picked up the club to deal with Ivar, smashing it into his knee. Ivar went down like a tree felled by an axe.

Then Gauk came at him with a knife, and Gunnar whipped round, barely noticing the slim blade slicing into his sleeve. He smashed the club into Gauk's elbow and his enemy sank to his knees, the colour draining from his face.

Gunnar stood over him, ready to strike again. Gauk flinched, his eyes wide with fear. But Gunnar lowered the club. "Just get out of my sight," he said.

Gauk scuttled away. The other two stumbled after him, Njal clutching his fingers, Ivar limping. Gunnar threw the club aside then turned to go, only to stop in his tracks once more. Rurik was leaning against a nearby hut.

"You look pleased with yourself," said Rurik. "That must have felt good. Although I see Gauk has left his mark." Rurik nodded at Gunnar's arm, where blood was staining the cloth.

"It's nothing," said Gunnar, not wanting to make any fuss.

Rurik frowned. "It will still need cleaning."

Back at the hut, Rurik quickly built up the fire and heated some water in a silver bowl. He added a sprinkle of aromatic dried herbs from a little bag he took out of the chest, then dampened a fine cloth in the fragrant water and gently cleaned Gunnar's wound, a shallow cut the length of a little finger. He carefully patted Gunnar's arm dry and tied another cloth round it.

"You'll live," said Rurik, ruffling the boy's hair. He went over to the door and emptied the bowl, chucking the water out into the alley. "At least till the next time you get into a fight. Although you weren't at all bad."

"You're good at this," said Gunnar, nodding at the neat bandage round his arm. He pulled on his tunic, making sure not to spoil Rurik's handiwork.

"You get to see a lot of wounds in my trade," said

Rurik. "And you learn to take care of your comrades, as they take care of you."

Gunnar studied the big man, and thought of the way Rurik had just salved his wound and ruffled his hair and practically called him a comrade. He hadn't seen any other slaves in Kaupang being treated like that by their masters. It seemed more the kind of thing a brother might do for a brother. Or a father for a son.

"Did you learn that when you were in Miklagard?" he said quietly.

Rurik glanced at him, surprised. "Who told you I've been to Miklagard?"

"Thorkel. I was talking to him earlier and it ... just sort of came up."

"Huh, I'll bet," snorted Rurik. "Thorkel gossips like an old woman."

"But is it true? Were you in the Greek Emperor's guard?"

"Why do you want to know?" Rurik threw a log on the fire. Sparks flew, the flames leaped higher. Shadows danced around them like ghosts.

"Because if it is, we have something in common. My father went to Miklagard, and he served in the Greek Emperor's guard too."

"Is that so? And when might that have been?"

"I'm not sure. I know he was back before I was born."

"Well, we could not have known each other, then," said Rurik, shaking his head. "I saw Miklagard for the first time five summers ago."

They fell silent for a moment. Gunnar was bitterly disappointed that this new piece of knowledge hadn't changed things. Rurik stared into the fire, his face closed, the way he looked when a black mood was about to settle on him. Now what? thought Gunnar. How could he build on his revelation, get Rurik to listen to him?

"What's Miklagard like?" he asked eventually. "Father never talked of it much, except to say the God Houses of the Christians are full of gold."

"The Greeks call them churches," muttered Rurik. "And I don't talk about those days much either. Not even to Thorkel when I'm drunk."

"Why is that? What happened to you in Miklagard?" Gunnar waited, but Rurik didn't answer. "What was it you said to me?" Gunnar went on. "Oh yes, *there's always a story to tell*, so maybe I can guess some of yours. You came here to forget something bad and you punish yourself for ending up as one of Orm's Hounds. That's why you have your black moods and get drunk."

Rurik scowled at him. "Take care, boy. Some men would kill you for speaking to them like that. My moods are not your business, or anyone else's. And why all this talk of your father? What do you want from me?"

"My freedom. And your help."

Rurik snorted. "To do what?"

"Avenge my father. He was murdered by raiders."

"So it seems both our lives are darkened by the shadow of the past. But if you want a man's help you must tell him the whole story."

"Then you must tell me yours. That's only fair."

"I'll be the one who decides what's fair, boy," said Rurik. "And this is not the moment for me to talk.

I will tell you my story only when I am ready."

Gunnar knew he was beaten, so he plunged into his tale. Rurik sat listening in silence. "I'll take your word for some of it," he said when Gunnar had finished. "I've seen halls burned, and that part of your story has the feel of truth. But the part about the Valkyries … can you prove you actually saw them?"

Gunnar looked at him, then lowered his gaze. "No, I can't."

"At least you're honest," said Rurik. "I've seen some strange things, but I've never seen a Valkyrie, and I've fought in my share of battles…"

"So you don't believe me," said Gunnar. "I swear it's all true!"

"That's not nearly enough, boy." Rurik stood up, his face closed off once more. "Now, I have a raging thirst I need to quench."

Gunnar watched his master go, and felt his heart fill with blackness.

# ELEVEN BLADE ON BLADE

WINTER DRAGGED ON, the sea freezing in the harbour, great dirty chunks of ice clunking against the thick pilings that held up the quayside. The days grew shorter, the nights longer and darker, and Gunnar sank to his lowest ebb.

106

It was Thorkel who kept him going, Thorkel who sought him out and made him eat and gave him his old sheepskin to wear when the cold bit even more deeply. Gunnar sometimes had the feeling he reminded Thorkel of somebody, and one day when they were in the crowded hall for supper he asked who it might be. Rurik was talking to Orm, Gunnar standing behind Thorkel as he ate.

"I had a son once," said Thorkel. "A fine boy who would have been about your age by now, had he lived. But he didn't, and neither did his mother. You've lost someone too – I can tell. Who was it? Mother, father? Both?"

"My father." Gunnar shrugged, unwilling to go into more detail.

"Death casts a shadow over us all," said Thorkel, spooning up broth from a wooden bowl. "There isn't a man or woman in here who hasn't been touched by it, or been its servant. The secret is not to give in to it until you have to."

"And when is that?" asked Gunnar.

"When you stop breathing, and not before."

"What about the Norns? Don't they decide our fate?"

"What if they do? You don't know when they're going to cut your thread, so you should carry on as if it's not going to happen. Otherwise you might just as well not have bothered to be born in the first place."

Rurik came over and sat down beside Thorkel. "A lot of people wish that about you, Thorkel. And why are you talking to the boy about fate and death? I'd rather you didn't make him any more miserable."

"You're lucky I like you, Rurik," said Thorkel, shaking his head. "Starkad is right – that tongue of yours is sure to get you killed some day."

"Well, one thing *I'm* sure of is that it won't be Starkad who'll do the killing," said Rurik. "Fetch me some more ale, Gunnar, there's a good lad."

Gunnar filled Rurik's goblet with ale from the big barrel in one corner of the hall. Starkad was at another table, watching Rurik, his eyes glittering with hate. Ari was there beside him, as were half a dozen other men, Starkad's band of supporters. Rurik took the goblet from Gunnar and raised it in a mock toast to Starkad, who did the same back. Thorkel tutted, and Rurik turned to him.

"You're such an old woman, Thorkel," he said. "What's wrong with a bit of healthy rivalry between men? Or should I say between a man and a fat boy?"

"Let's hope it doesn't get unhealthy then," said Thorkel. "You know as well as I do where this kind of thing ends, Rurik. If I were you I'd stay away from dark alleys. You might be the better warrior, but hatred leads to cunning."

Rurik shrugged, and Gunnar suddenly realized the big man didn't care whether he lived or died. Gunnar understood that feeling now, and he guessed that it made a warrior like Rurik a very dangerous man to be around.

The days passed slowly. Spring arrived at last with a warm wind from the south, and the iron ruts in Kaupang's alleys soon became the same old stinking mud. The sea ice melted and the harbour grew busier. Trading ships appeared first, then the longships came, many of them bringing slaves for Orm, and his pens were soon full again. Gunnar was afraid to look into them sometimes, half expecting to see faces he recognized, people from his own steading.

Then one morning he heard something that made his heart race. Rurik was in a black mood, and Gunnar was hanging around the quayside. He passed a longship where two men were mending sails, talking while they worked their needles.

"I'd never seen anything like it," said one of them, a gingery man with a scrappy beard. "Mountains of ice that slide across the land and crush rocks to powder. Rivers of fire that burst out of giant cracks beneath your feet."

"Sounds like a hard place to live," said the other, a dark, wiry man with several of his front teeth missing. "What did you say it was called?"

"It's got a couple of names," said the first man. "The Land of Ice and Fire, or just Iceland. It's not that bad, though. There's good land to farm too."

So the Land of Ice and Fire *did* exist! Gunnar asked Thorkel about what he had heard, wishing he had done so before. Soon he knew it took a month by sea to get there, as the old man had said. From then on Gunnar spent every spare moment on the quayside, wondering if he could stow away on a longship.

A few days later, Rurik set off to the hall for supper with Gunnar as usual. The setting sun was a red ball and night was starting to fill the town with darkness, but the air was still warm and seagulls swooped and squawked above the roofs. After a while Rurik and Gunnar came to a crossroads and stopped. Three men blocked the way ahead, the sun outlining them with a fiery glow.

It was Starkad, flanked on one side by Ari and on the other by Hogni, their faces grim. Starkad and Ari were wearing chainmail and helmets. They carried shields and had drawn their swords. Hogni was also wearing chainmail, a rusty old byrnie with big, ragged holes in it that was far too short for him. He carried an old short-handled battle-axe, its blade a thick slab of black iron.

"So, the moment has come," Rurik said, hand on his sword hilt. "Is it to be just you and me, Starkad, or do I have to kill your two puppies as well?"

"You'll have to kill the whole pack, Rurik," said Starkad, a smile on his lips. "You don't seem to have many friends among the men of Orm's hall."

Gunnar looked round and drew in his breath. Starkad's supporters blocked each alley, half a dozen of Orm's Hounds armed and ready for battle.

But Rurik just laughed. "You call that lot *men*?" he snorted. "And where did you get that byrnie, Hogni? You should have stolen one that was a better fit."

"You think you're so funny, Rurik, don't you?" said Hogni, his face dark with anger. "Well, you won't be laughing much after I've finished with you. And then I'm going to kill that slave boy of yours as slowly as I can."

"You won't be killing anyone today," Rurik said quietly, slowly drawing his sword from the scabbard. "Give me some room, Gunnar."

Suddenly Ari rushed forward with a yell, wildly swinging his sword. Rurik simply stepped to one side and Ari stumbled past, flailing. Two more men moved forward, their swords raised, and Rurik parried huge blows from both, blade ringing on blade. Rurik soon killed one man, almost hacking his neck through, and wounded the other in the shoulder, forcing him to back off.

"Come on then, Hogni!" said Rurik, laughing. "What are you waiting for?"

Hogni roared and came at him, his axe held high. Rurik's sword flashed, and Gunnar glimpsed a look of terror on the smith's face. Then Hogni was dead too, his body sprawled at Rurik's feet, his head split wide open.

"What about you, Starkad?" said Rurik. You haven't struck a blow yet. But then maybe you're a coward who watches while others do the fighting."

Now Starkad stepped forward and rained blows on Rurik, who parried every strike. Starkad was soon gasping for breath, his face red with effort.

"You'll have to do better than that," said Rurik, enjoying himself.

Gunnar realized Ari was sneaking up behind Rurik. "Watch out, Rurik!" he yelled, and Rurik looked round. Starkad saw that Rurik was distracted and came in for the kill. But Rurik quickly turned back to deal with him, ramming his sword deep into his chest. Rurik pulled his blade free and Starkad sank to his knees, looking surprised, then fell face down in the mud.

Ari roared at the others and they charged, shields overlapping, a wooden wave that crashed into Rurik and knocked him down. They held him on the ground as Ari stood over him, his sword point at Rurik's throat.

"I could kill you here," Ari hissed. "But I think that pleasure should belong to someone else. Take him to Orm – and bring the boy!"

# TWELVE
# A SLAVE'S
# DEATH

ONCE MORE GUNNAR was dragged through the alleys and made to kneel before the King of Kaupang in his dark hall. Rurik kneeled beside him, stripped of his sword and chainmail, blood running down his face from a gash where an iron shield rim had struck his forehead. Both had their wrists tied behind their backs.

Ari stood over them with his sword drawn, and a crowd had gathered in the hall. Starkad's corpse was laid out on a table near by. Vigdis had wailed when he had been brought in and flung herself on the body, but now she stood in front of Rurik and Gunnar.

"Somebody give me a knife!" she screeched. She spat in Rurik's face, then did the same to Gunnar. "I'll butcher the pair of them like pigs at the autumn slaughtering," she hissed. "They killed my son, my Starkad!"

"Enough, woman," Orm growled. He was sitting on his throne. "You never had a good word to say about Starkad while he was alive."

"What are you talking about?" Vigdis screamed, rounding on her husband. "You were the one who ran him down, saying he was too rash!"

"And he proved it by getting himself killed," rumbled Orm. "He was a fool to think he could fight Rurik. I told him, but he wouldn't listen."

"Is that it, then?" screeched Vigdis. "It was Starkad's fault, so you're going to let your precious Rurik get

116

away with murdering him? He was our *son*!"

"I know that as well as you do, Vigdis," said Orm. "I'm not going to let Rurik get away with anything. He must pay for what he's done."

"What does that mean?" said Vigdis. "I want to see him die slowly."

"Oh, he's going to die," said Orm. "But he owes me compensation. Pay me the blood price for my son, Rurik, and I will make sure your death is swift and painless. How much Greek silver do you have hidden away?"

Gunnar glanced at the big man kneeling beside him. Rurik smiled but didn't reply to Orm, and Ari prodded his shoulder with the end of his sword.

"Your master is waiting for an answer," he snapped. "Speak up."

Rurik looked coolly at Ari, then turned to Orm. "I don't have any more silver arm rings, if that's what you mean," he said. "Not that Starkad was worth one."

"So my son was worth less than a slave boy," growled Orm.

Rurik shrugged. Vigdis spat in his face once more,

117

and Rurik laughed at her. Gunnar glimpsed Thorkel looking on from the crowd. Thorkel gave a slight shake of the head, and Gunnar knew he was saying he couldn't help.

"We should just cut their throats and be done with it," said Ari.

"Not the boy," said Orm. "I might get something for him."

"Maybe so…" said Ari. "But your son would still be alive if the boy hadn't distracted him. Starkad was more than holding his own till then."

"Liar!" Gunnar yelled. "He would never have beaten Rurik and you know it. You were sneaking up behind Rurik to stab him in the back!"

Ari hit him hard with his free hand, knocking him sideways. Pain shot through Gunnar's head and his cheek throbbed as he lay on the floor.

"Very well," said Orm. "The boy dies too. Take them down to the harbour. One of them is a slave, and the other can die a slave's death."

"That's more like it," said Vigdis, cackling. "I'm going to enjoy this."

Gunnar was pulled to his feet and dragged out of the hall with Rurik, as the crowd swarmed round them. Ari led the procession through the dark alleys with a flaming torch held high, Vigdis beside him. At one point an old man emerged from an alley and nearly bumped into them.

"Forgive me," said the old man. "I didn't mean to get in your way."

"Move aside, you old fool!" Ari yelled, roughly pushing past him.

The old man did as he was told, but not before Gunnar felt something being pressed into his hand. It was a small knife – and suddenly he remembered the bone-handled blade the old man had used at the God House.

Gunnar tried to look over his shoulder, straining against the men holding him. Had it been the same old man? And what was he supposed to do with such a small knife? It wouldn't be any good as a weapon. He might be able to cut the binding on his wrists with it, but he was surrounded and wouldn't have a hope of escaping. He would have to bide his time, wait for a better opportunity.

"You men, fetch more torches!" yelled Ari at last.

They had reached the harbour. The tide was out and mud stretched beyond the ships to the drowning posts. Gunnar glanced at Rurik again. The big man was smiling with his eyes closed. "Rurik!" Gunnar hissed at him. *"Rurik!"*

"He isn't listening, boy," said Ari. "He's halfway to the afterlife already. Hurry up, lads, let's get them lashed to the posts. The tide will turn soon."

A couple of men shoved Gunnar and Rurik off the quayside. They landed in the mud and Gunnar's breath was driven from his body. He held on to the knife though, keeping it hidden in his clenched fist while a couple of men lashed him and Rurik to the posts. "Well, Rurik, are you ready to die?" Ari shouted from the quayside. "Any last words for us? Or has your wit finally failed you?"

Gunnar looked up at Ari and Vigdis and the crowd. He thought about the knife again and turned it over in his hand. He would have to wait until he was under the water to cut himself free. What then?

There was a crowd watching, so he'd have to swim off underwater to escape. But where could he go? If he headed out to sea he'd drown just the same. And what about Rurik?

"Well, there's one good thing about dying, Ari," said Rurik. "At least after tonight I won't ever have to look at your ugly face again."

There was a great roar of laughter from the crowd, and Ari scowled. "I should have killed you when I had the chance!" he yelled.

"You mean when four men were holding me down?" said Rurik. "They're lucky you didn't try. You'd probably have killed one of them instead!"

The laughter was louder this time, and Ari scowled so fiercely it looked as if his face was folding in on itself. But then Gunnar saw the old man from the God House standing just behind Ari, smiling beneath his wide-brimmed hat. Gunnar felt the hairs on the back of his neck stand up. So it *had* been him!

"I've a good mind to come back down there and kill you now," Ari yelled.

"Don't you dare, Ari!" screamed Vigdis. "Orm said he was to drown!"

"Don't argue with her, Ari," said Rurik. "She'll take your other ear off."

The crowd roared again, but Gunnar was watching the old man. He moved forward, peered over the quayside, then sought Gunnar's eyes. Of course – the quayside was supported by thick pilings, and behind them was a space which the sea never filled, however high the tide. If they could swim there underwater no one would see them from above, and they could wait till the crowd had gone.

"The tide's coming in!" someone yelled, and the crowd cheered.

Gunnar looked down. Sea water was rolling over the mud, making pools that swiftly overflowed. Soon it was up to his ankles, and rising steadily.

# THIRTEEN
# FOOD FOR
# THE FISHES

G UNNAR BEGAN SAWING
at the bonds on his wrists,
and soon his hands were
free. Dealing with the rope
round his chest would be
harder. He would have to
wait till the sea covered it.

And he still had to work out what to do about Rurik.

"I'm sorry, Gunnar," Rurik said suddenly. "You don't deserve to die like this."

"I don't intend to," muttered Gunnar. The ships in the harbour stirred and creaked. Small waves slapped against their hulls, and the sea chuckled under their keels. Up on the quayside the crowd grew even noisier, and the old man from the God House had disappeared.

"You must try to accept it, Gunnar." Rurik's voice was soft and sad. "This is our fate. It seems neither of us will be going to Valhalla."

"But I can save us, Rurik. I've got a knife."

"I should have died a warrior's death..." Rurik said wistfully. "Do you really want to know what happened to me in Miklagard?"

Gunnar groaned in frustration. He wanted to yell and scream at Rurik and shock him out of his despair. They didn't have time to worry about such things – the tide was coming in quickly and the water was already up to Gunnar's waist. But Rurik's story might be important. "I'm listening," Gunnar said.

"I betrayed my brother," said Rurik. "We had always been close – only two summers separated us. So we took the road to Miklagard together, and as I was the older I swore an oath that I would look after him. We fought the Greek Emperor's enemies many times side by side. But on the day he was cut down by barbarian raiders I was sleeping off the ale I had drunk the night before."

"That wasn't a betrayal. You might not have been able to save him."

"Maybe so," Rurik said quietly, his head down. "But I should have been there. I would have died to protect him, I swear."

Neither of them spoke for a moment, both lost in their own thoughts.

"We do have a lot in common, you and I," Gunnar said after a while. "You punish yourself because you believe you let your brother down. I do the same because I did nothing while raiders killed my father."

Rurik turned to look at him. "But there was nothing you could have done. They were warriors and you were a boy."

"What does that matter? Like you, I can never forgive myself."

A rock splashed into the sea between them. "Hey, stop all that whispering!" Ari yelled. "You should be doing less talking – and more drowning!" Ari grinned, pleased with his joke, and the crowd laughed with him. Rurik looked up at them, but said nothing.

"What was your brother's name, Rurik?" said Gunnar, his teeth chattering. "Do you think he would have wanted you to die a slave's death? Somehow I doubt it. You swore an oath to him that you didn't fulfil. You can make up for that by helping me fulfil mine. But only if you live."

Rurik frowned, then closed his eyes. After a moment he opened them and turned to gaze at Gunnar again. "Did I hear you say you have a knife?" he said. "Where did you get it?"

"That's not important," Gunnar said. "I'll cut myself free as soon as the water covers me. I'll stay under and free you, then hide beneath the quayside. You can follow as soon as the water covers you too. Once the crowd has gone we'll make good our escape, get

128

out of this stinking town for ever."

Rurik shook his head and laughed gently. "Ah, Gunnar, how full of courage and cleverness you are! Most grown men would have given up long since, but you keep fighting. Who am I to argue? We'll probably drown, but I'll try your plan. For your sake, and my brother's…"

But Gunnar had stopped listening and was already hacking at the rope round his chest. They were running out of time. The water had reached the level of his shoulders and was lapping at his chin. Soon it reached his nose, and he just managed to cut himself loose as the waves swept over his head.

The crowd cheered, but the sea roared in his ears and their noise vanished. It was dark under the water and he felt afraid that he might not even be able to find Rurik. The current tugged at him, but Gunnar reached out in what felt like the right direction and found the big man's arm. He held on to Rurik's post with one hand, sawing at his bonds with the other.

He cut through them at last, then turned to swim towards the quayside. He kicked out, his chest bursting, and had almost started to panic when his hand touched something hard covered in slimy seaweed – one of the pilings.

He pulled himself round it and shot up, bursting through the surface and gulping in a huge breath, the knife slipping from his hand. More pilings stood to his right and left, and an arm's length above his head was the quayside. Stray gleams of light from the crowd's torches stabbed down through the narrow gaps between the planks. They were still cheering and jeering, and suddenly Gunnar heard the unmistakable voice of Vigdis. "There he goes!" she screeched.

Gunnar whipped round. Rurik was struggling to keep his head above the water. As Gunnar watched, the big man took one last, desperate gulp of air – and then the sea claimed him, leaving only bubbles and foam.

The crowd gave the biggest cheer so far. Gunnar stared out over the waves, praying that Rurik was swimming towards him below the surface. But he didn't appear and Gunnar began to worry. How long had it taken to cover the distance from the posts to the quayside? Surely Rurik should have made it by now. Perhaps he hadn't cut all the ropes. Perhaps Rurik was already dead...

"Well, that's the end of them," Gunnar heard Ari say. "They're both food for the fishes now, and good riddance."

Come on, Rurik, thought Gunnar, where are you? Suddenly a dark shape rose from the water beside him. It was Rurik, and the big man took a deep breath and squeezed Gunnar's shoulder. Above them people laughed and called out to one another, but it was clear the crowd was leaving. When it seemed that everyone had gone, Gunnar made as if to head for the quayside steps. Rurik held him back.

"Wait," Rurik hissed. There was a sudden flare of light and Gunnar saw that somebody was directly above them. He looked up through the planking – and drew in his breath sharply. Ari was holding a torch out over the water.

Gunnar's heart pounded. What if Ari had guessed what they'd done? But Ari walked away at last, his heavy footsteps echoing in the space beneath the quayside, and Gunnar breathed out. Rurik squeezed his shoulder again, and they made for the steps. Rurik hauled Gunnar up beside him, and they lay there gasping like a pair of dying salmon in the bottom of a fisherman's boat.

After a while Gunnar sensed a light above them and raised his eyes. A dark figure was standing at the top of the steps, a man holding a torch, his face in shadow. Gunnar groaned again, sure Ari had found them.

# FOURTEEN
## A FINE-LOOKING
# CRAFT

GUNNAR WAITED FOR Ari to yell, for the alarm to be raised. But it wasn't Ari – it was Thorkel.

"Quickly now, come with me," Thorkel said, and reached out a hand.

Gunnar didn't stop to ask questions. He

scrambled up the steps, Rurik behind him. Soon Thorkel was hurrying them across the empty quayside and through the dark alleys to his own hut, dousing the torch in a barrel of water outside and pushing them through the door. He lit an oil lamp and hung it on a rafter, its pale glow chasing shadows into the corners.

"How did you know we weren't dead?" said Gunnar.

"I didn't," said Thorkel. "I came just in case, and you appeared at my feet. You nearly frightened *me* to death." He opened a chest, pulled out a couple of tunics and tossed them to Gunnar and Rurik. "You'd better get out of those wet clothes. If the Gods are willing, you could be in the mountains before the sun rises and people wonder why you're not still tied to those posts."

"No," said Gunnar. "I'm not going to the mountains."

"But you have to get out of Kaupang!" said Thorkel. "You can't hide from Orm for long, and he'll think of an even worse way to kill you next time."

"I know all that," said Gunnar. "But the only way I'm leaving Kaupang is by sea. I have an oath to fulfil, and I want you to find someone who will give me passage to the Land of Ice and Fire. Rurik is coming, and so should you."

"What in Odin's name is the boy talking about, Rurik?"

"It's a long story," sighed Rurik. "You should just do what he says."

Thorkel scowled. "I'm too old to go voyaging," he said, shaking his head. "But I'll do what I can. Although finding anybody who's mad enough to take the pair of you out of Kaupang on a ship won't be easy."

Gunnar smiled. "You know who to ask though, don't you?"

"You're right, I do…" Thorkel said, rubbing his beard. "Mind you, I have a feeling the ship I'm thinking of will be leaving very soon."

"We'd best get on with it then, hadn't we?" said Rurik.

Thorkel nodded, opened the hut door and re-lit

his torch. "I'll make the introduction. After that you're on your own."

Soon they were hurrying through the alleys again. They saw no one at first, but then they turned a corner and bumped into a couple of Orm's Hounds.

"Is that you, Thorkel?" said one of the men. His gaze moved to Gunnar and Rurik, and his eyes widened. "Hey, you two are supposed to be dead..." They both grabbed their sword hilts, but Thorkel beat them to it, drawing his blade in one deft movement. He swiftly chopped down the man who had spoken, but the other dodged his blade and ran off like a frightened hare.

"That's done it," said Thorkel, sheathing his sword, his face grim. "Now Orm will send every man in his hall to track you down."

"What if they can't get out of the hall?" said Gunnar. "We could block the doors somehow. We could set fire to the roof as well."

Rurik looked at Gunnar and raised his eyebrows. "It's worth a try," he said. "That would certainly keep them busy for a while."

"Well, let's get on with it," Thorkel muttered. "Since we've been spotted together I'm going to have to come with you after all."

Orm's hall was in darkness, but the doors were partially open and they could hear raised voices. Rurik ducked into the porch and emerged with half a dozen spears from the rack. He closed the doors and rammed the spears through the handles, bracing the shafts against the doorposts.

Then he took Thorkel's torch and handed it to Gunnar. "It works best if you set the fire in several places," he said. "Although you probably know that."

Thorkel gave them both a puzzled look, but Gunnar ignored him. The smell of smoke and the fierce heat sent his mind back to the night his home had been destroyed. He loved the idea of setting fire to Orm's hall, of making him and the others in there suffer, if only for a little while. He wished he could unlock Orm's pens and let all his slaves out as well, but he knew that was impossible. So he walked the length of the hall, thrusting the torch into the thatch.

"Time to go," said Thorkel. Gunnar threw the torch as far as he could onto the roof and looked over his shoulder as they hurried away. The thatch was already burning strongly, and someone was banging at the doors from inside.

Thorkel took Gunnar and Rurik to a ship at the far end of the harbour. There were enough torches on this part of the quayside for Gunnar to see it was a fine-looking craft, a lean warship with a tall carved prow. He had also witnessed enough sailings from Kaupang to know it was on the point of leaving. The crew – perhaps thirty men in all – were sitting at the benches holding their oars.

"Hey, Viglaf, glad we caught you," said Thorkel, looking down into the ship from the quayside, his voice light and easy. "I've come to collect that favour you owe me. I want passage out of here for me and my companions."

A short, stocky man looked up at them from the stern of the ship. He had on a red cap, and the sides of his head were as smooth and white as a duck's egg.

"Is that so?" Viglaf said. "I can't deny I owe you a

138

favour, Thorkel, but isn't this a bit sudden? You didn't mention anything about it when we spoke last."

"Well, you know how it is," said Thorkel. "You can have enough of being in one place, and we've had our fill of Kaupang. So can we come aboard?"

"But you don't even know where we're going," said Viglaf, a look of deep suspicion stealing onto his face. "I'm sure I didn't tell you. And who are the other two? I've seen the big man before. Isn't he one of Orm's Hounds?"

There was movement further down the ship. A crewman was standing on his rowing bench, gesturing at the town and saying something. Gunnar turned to look in the direction he was pointing. A fiery glow lit the sky over the roofs of the huts. Bright flames were leaping, and there was shouting as well.

"I'm a friend of Thorkel's, and the boy is my slave," said Rurik. "We don't care where you're going, so long as you take us out of this stinking hole."

"It might not stink so much once it burns down," muttered Viglaf. "Is that anything to do with you?" he said, nodding in the direction of the flames.

The shouting was growing louder, and there were screams of panic as well.

"No, of course not!" said Thorkel, shrugging. "Why would it be?"

"What kind of a fool do you think I am, Thorkel?" said Viglaf. "I can add two and two. You turn up suddenly wanting to get out of Kaupang at the same moment that Orm's hall goes up in flames. Something else was going on earlier, dark deeds for all I know. I kept my men out of it because I don't want any trouble, not in Kaupang. I don't want to make Orm into an enemy."

"All right, Viglaf," said Thorkel. "I'll admit we're not exactly Orm's favourite people, but it's not as bad as it looks. I can explain everything, I promise."

"Sorry, Thorkel," said Viglaf. "Now, I have a ship to get under way..."

"You might want to think again," said Thorkel, his voice suddenly cold and hard. "Just talking to us like this is probably enough to make you an enemy of Orm's. And if he catches us I'll tell him it was your idea to burn his hall."

Gunnar looked at Thorkel, impressed. It was a bold gamble, and Gunnar half expected Viglaf to laugh and order his crew to seize them as a gift for Orm. But Thorkel clearly knew his man. Viglaf scowled and was silent for a moment. "Very well, you can come aboard," he muttered at last, looking nervously up and down the empty quayside. "But don't think I'm happy about it, Thorkel."

"You're never happy about anything," said Thorkel, jumping down into the ship with Rurik and Gunnar. "Least of all missing an ebb tide, if I recall."

Viglaf gave him a sour glare, then pointedly turned away. "Crew of the *Sea Eagle*, cast off fore and aft! Out with your oars… Erlend, call the beat…"

The *Sea Eagle*… thought Gunnar. The ship moved out of the harbour, thirty oars striking the dark waters, taking him away from Kaupang. But all he could think of was the prophecy the old man had made at the God House:

*You will fly with the eagle to the Land of Ice and Fire…*

# FIFTEEN
## THE EAGLE
# FEATHER

THE RED GLOW over Kaupang remained visible behind them till the rising sun swallowed it. There was a strong breeze, and Viglaf gave the order to ship oars and run out the sail. Like a hound let off the leash to hunt, the *Sea Eagle* leaped forward and cast up

142

glittering arcs of water as it cut through the waves.

Gunnar stood by the gunwale in the bows of the ship, relishing the fresh air, the cool spray on his face, the tang of salt. He looked at the prow beside him, the upwardly curving post carved into the likeness of a great eagle.

"I'm sorry, Gunnar," Thorkel was saying. "I just don't believe it. Perhaps seeing your father killed did something to your mind. That can happen."

"You're right," said Rurik. "But I've been thinking about this old man he says he met. Doesn't the boy's description of him sound oddly familiar to you?"

Thorkel nodded and shrugged. "Maybe. Odin is sometimes described like that in the old stories. But it still doesn't prove what the boy says. Somebody might have put the idea in his head. He might even have dreamed the whole thing."

Odin? thought Gunnar. Could it be true? Was it Odin who had helped set him on the road to Valhalla? Who had slipped him a knife so he could save his own life and Rurik's? Gunnar had prayed to Odin for help, and he had known there was something strange

143

about the old man from the moment he had met him.

Thorkel and Rurik were still talking, but Gunnar had stopped listening. He reached into the pocket of his leggings and pulled out the feather the old man – Odin – had left for him. He had nearly lost it several times, and it was bent and bedraggled, its spine broken. Odin had told him he would *fly with the eagle to the Land of Ice and Fire*, and here he was on a ship called the *Sea Eagle*. Was the feather just a symbol of that, or did it mean something more?

He caught a movement in the air from the corner of his eye. A pair of gulls hovered above the waves just beside the *Sea Eagle*, almost near enough for him to reach out and touch. They squawked at him, and he remembered the noisy crows at the God House and the magpies on the roof of Hogni's smithy.

"Thorkel, in the old stories, does Odin have a pair of birds?" he said.

"Yes, Hugin and Munin – the names mean *thought* and *memory*. They're ravens, although sometimes they take other forms. Why do you ask?"

Gunnar nodded at the gulls. "I'm sure Odin is

keeping an eye on me," he said. Thorkel gave the birds a surprised look, but then Viglaf appeared.

"We need to talk, Thorkel," he said.

"What about?" sighed Thorkel.

"I owed you a favour, and you wanted me to sneak you and your friends out of Kaupang," said Viglaf with a shrug. "Well, I've done that, but I swear the sooner I'm rid of you the happier I'll be. I'll put you ashore in Gokstad."

"That's not far enough," said Thorkel. "It's only a day from Kaupang."

"Tough luck," said Viglaf. "This time my mind is made up."

"Well, maybe we could make you change it," Rurik said softly. He towered over Viglaf and stared down at him, his face stony. Viglaf didn't flinch.

"You could try," he said. "You're a big man and you look like you can fight. I know Thorkel can be handy in a scrap too. But you don't have any weapons, and there's only the two of you, not counting the slave boy, obviously."

Three of Viglaf's men were close behind him,

swords unsheathed. Beyond them Gunnar saw the rest of the crew standing by their benches, swords on their hips or spears in easy reach, their eyes fixed on the group in the bows.

"Now let's just try to keep things calm," said Thorkel, his hand on Rurik's forearm. "We're all friends here, so I'm sure we can work this out."

Gunnar could see Viglaf wasn't convinced, even when Thorkel reached into his tunic and pulled out a purse that chinked with gold and silver. Suddenly Gunnar felt a surge of anger flooding through him – here he was yet again with strangers deciding his future. He would tell *them* where he wanted to go.

"You will take me to the Land of Ice and Fire, Viglaf," he said, stepping forward and looking him in the eye. "I will go nowhere else, do you hear?"

"Shut your mouth," said Viglaf. "I don't take orders from a slave."

"I apologize for him, Viglaf," Thorkel was saying. "He doesn't—"

Then he stopped talking, his eyes wide – for the feather in Gunnar's hand had begun to glow with a strange light. Gunnar wasn't surprised. Deep down he had known all along there was more magic to come. He even knew what to do – he pressed the feather against the prow and watched it merge into the wood. There was a brief moment of stillness, then real feathers appeared as the carving came to life. Soon the eagle was rolling its great head and stretching its wings, almost as if it were trying to get the wooden stiffness out of its body.

Finally it turned, whipping round to screech at Viglaf and his crew.

Viglaf recoiled, crashing into the men behind him. The rest of the crew were equally startled. Some ran for the stern, others dived behind the benches, a few retreated with swords raised or spears held out.

Thorkel had backed off too. Only Rurik didn't move. He shook his head in wonderment. "I'm impressed, Gunnar," he said. "That's quite a trick."

Viglaf slowly stood up. The eagle studied him, its great head cocked to one side as if it were trying to work out whether he might be good to eat.

"I've voyaged on every sea and seen strange things in many lands," muttered Viglaf. "But I've never seen anything like this. Are you a sorcerer, boy?"

"Perhaps I am," said Gunnar. "Or perhaps I'm just a boy who needs to fulfil an oath he swore. Now will you take me to the Land of Ice and Fire?"

"If it's Iceland you mean," Viglaf said cautiously, "we'd need to go west, and we're supposed to be heading east, back into the Baltic…" The eagle screeched more loudly this time. Viglaf ducked behind a bench. "All right!" he yelled. "I'll take you wherever you like! What else do you want?"

"Since you ask," said Rurik, "you can take his thrall ring off." Gunnar turned to stare at his master, and the big man returned his gaze. Neither of them spoke.

"Fine," said Viglaf. "But first he can turn that thing back into a prow."

Gunnar looked at the eagle, unsure what to do. He thought for a moment, then put his hand on the spot where he had placed the feather. Immediately the eagle turned to face the sea once more. Gunnar felt the magical life flowing out of it until at last the same bedraggled feather lay in his palm. He laughed, and the gulls hovering over the waves seemed to squawk with pleasure too.

Gunnar sat on a chest in the middle of the ship. One of Viglaf's men, a young, red-haired Viking called Erlend, worked nervously on the thrall ring with a file. Thorkel and Rurik stood looking on, arms folded. Viglaf and the rest of the crew had retreated to the stern for the time being and watched from there.

"The join is broken," said Erlend at last. He gripped the ring, getting his hands between it and Gunnar's neck, but he couldn't pull it open.

"Here, let me," Rurik said. He took the ring in his hands and stretched it wide, as if nothing could be easier. Then he handed it to Gunnar. "You are no longer a slave, Gunnar," he said. "I give you your freedom."

Gunnar stared down at the twisted piece of metal. After a moment he raised his eyes to Rurik. "I owe you a silver arm ring for this, don't I?"

"Not any more. You paid your debt when you saved my life."

Gunnar rubbed his neck, then rose to his feet and went over to the gunwale. He remembered his months as a slave, all the curses and kicks, all the insults he had endured. Then he threw the thrall ring as far as he could, watching it spin through the spray-filled air and plunge into the sea with a small splash.

The ship skimmed across the waves towards Iceland – and Valhalla.

# SIXTEEN
## DARK BLOOD
## FLOWING

**THEY HUGGED THE** coastline for the first few days, then Viglaf turned the *Sea Eagle* westwards, out into the open sea. He and his crew were wary of Gunnar at first, but their fear soon wore off when he didn't perform any more sorcery.

One night Gunnar was sitting with Rurik. Viglaf had left Erlend at the steerboard and was playing a game of knuckle-bones with Thorkel amidships, and most of the others were asleep. A light breeze filled the sail, the sea gently hissing by beneath the hull. It was summer now, and the sky was never fully dark, the horizon lined with a faint glow even in the middle of the night.

"I've been thinking, Rurik," said Gunnar. "I know Odin has helped me, but he hasn't exactly made things easy, has he? Why did he let Gauk sell me as a slave? Why did I have to spend more than half a year in Kaupang?"

"The Gods cannot live your life for you, Gunnar," said Rurik. "A man must deal with whatever his fate throws at him. Be thankful Odin has helped you so far, and that he might help you again. In the meantime you must do what you can to help yourself, as you already have done, and bravely, too."

"But what if I can't fulfil my oath? What if I fail?" It was the question that filled Gunnar's daytime thoughts and haunted his dreams at night.

"What if you don't?" said Rurik, grinning. "A boy journeying to Valhalla and bringing his father back from the dead? Now that will be a tale to tell! The skalds will make poems about it that will be sung till the day of Ragnarok! I can almost hear it now, 'The Saga of Gunnar the Fierce'." Rurik began to chant in the way that skalds sang their verses, his deep voice rising and falling.

> *"He came to the steading*
> *Gunnar of the stern gaze*
> *And slew his fearful foes*
> *His bright blade flashing*
> *A lightning bolt for a warrior*
> *The dark blood flowing..."*

Gunnar stared at Rurik, amazed to hear such powerful words coming from his mouth. But he loved the image it had created in his mind, that of Gunnar the Fierce, relentless in his quest for vengeance, the heads of his enemies rolling before him. "I didn't know you were a skald, Rurik," he said, smiling.

"He isn't much of one," grunted Thorkel, who had come to join them. "Listen, Gunnar, I want to talk to you. We need to be practical. Taking your revenge on this Skuli isn't going to be easy, even if Odin agrees to let your father out of Valhalla. However good a warrior your father is, he'll need some men."

"He's a *great* warrior," said Gunnar. "And he'll have you and Rurik, won't he?" Gunnar almost said that he would be beside them too, but he knew it wouldn't matter if he was there. What was it Father had said the night Skuli had come to the steading – *this will be men's work*? And he was still a boy.

"Even great warriors sometimes need help, Gunnar," said Rurik.

"What about Viglaf and his crew?" said Thorkel. "They certainly know how to fight. Maybe Odin led you to the *Sea Eagle* for that very reason."

"Do you think so? Viglaf doesn't seem to like us much."

"Viglaf can be a grumpy oaf," Thorkel said with a wry smile. "And liking us is neither here nor there. He's a Viking, and if he believes there's gold to be had

156

in an adventure, he'll be right behind you. He was awed by your sorcery with the prow, and I'm sure he could be persuaded to help you and your father."

"What was he doing in Kaupang?" Gunnar asked.

"You mean was he there to sell slaves?" said Thorkel. "Not this time. He came to buy food, fill his water barrels, give his men a few days on land before they go raiding again. But I'd be lying if I told you Viglaf never took captives to sell as slaves. It's a rare Viking who doesn't if there's a profit to be had."

Gunnar frowned and turned to Rurik. The big man shrugged.

"Beggars can't be choosers, Gunnar," he said. "A wise warrior uses the weapons to hand, even if they're not as good as the ones he'd like."

Gunnar thought for a moment, then he shrugged too. "Will you speak to him, Thorkel?" he asked. "I can offer him glory, but not gold. Not yet, anyway."

"We don't have to tell him that," said Thorkel, winking. "Hey, Viglaf…"

Gunnar watched Thorkel go, but his mind was full of fighting, images of blades rising and falling, Skuli and Grim and all the Wolf Men paying with their lives for the evil they had done. Then he lay down to sleep, smiling fiercely, wishing that he could truly be the avenging Gunnar of Rurik's poem.

Three days later they turned north and the sea grew grey, the sun hiding behind black clouds. Then one morning Gunnar woke to a world of hushed voices and quiet splashing. The *Sea Eagle* was surrounded by a mist so thick it was impossible to see the ship's prow from the stern. Gunnar threw off the furs he had been wrapped in and made his way forward. Rurik and Thorkel were already by the prow, peering into the mist, Viglaf close beside them.

"What's happening?" whispered Gunnar. The sail had been furled, and the crew were at their benches, gently dipping and raising their oars.

"Viglaf thinks there's land ahead," said Thorkel. "But we don't know how far because of the mist and we have to take it slowly, in case of rocks."

"Is it the Land of Ice and Fire?" said Gunnar.

"It had better be, or we're badly lost," growled

Viglaf. He turned and yelled, looking upwards and cupping his hands round his mouth. "Can you see anything yet, Einar?" Viglaf had a loud voice, but the mist seemed to deaden it.

"Just mist and more mist," replied Einar Squint-Eye, Viglaf's best look-out man. He was clinging to the top of the mast. "Wait, I think it's clearing…"

Gunnar felt the breeze stirring. The mist ahead started to swirl and they all leaned forward, straining their eyes to see something, anything.

"Steady as she goes, lads," growled Viglaf. "Somebody tell Erlend to put us on a straight course." More voices relayed Viglaf's order to Erlend in the stern, and Gunnar felt the *Sea Eagle* twitch as Erlend moved the steerboard.

Suddenly the breeze strengthened and tore gaps in the mist. Gunnar glimpsed massive, dark shapes looming in the distance. It was a chain of mountains, their peaks covered in snow, huge glaciers gripping their flanks. Below them lay a jagged shoreline of rocks and cliffs with skirts of seething white foam.

"Well, that looks like Iceland to me," said Viglaf,

turning to Gunnar. "Is there a particular place you want to go? Most of the settlements are on the coast."

Gunnar felt the eyes of all three men on him. He hadn't thought about where in the Land of Ice and Fire he would find Bifrost, but he was sure Odin would somehow show him where to go.

"Just take us to wherever it's easy to land," he said. "But not near a settlement. I want to stay as far away from people as possible."

"I can understand that," grunted Thorkel. "Do as the boy says, Viglaf."

Viglaf ordered Erlend to follow the coastline. Soon the mist had gone and the wind grew strong enough for them to raise the sail. Gunnar stood by the prow, studying the shore, looking for any kind of sign, perhaps even Odin himself. But there was nothing, and the only creatures Gunnar saw were crowds of wheeling, screeching gulls, none of them remotely interested in him.

"Hey, Viglaf!" yelled Einar Squint-Eye after a while. "A beach, over there!"

Viglaf peered in the direction Einar was pointing.

160

"Seems as good a place as any," Viglaf said with a shrug. "Right, lads, let's take her in. Steady now."

Moments later the keel of the *Sea Eagle* crunched onto the beach and they came to a halt. Rurik jumped down from the gunwale beside the prow and landed in the sea, the water over his knees. He looked up at Gunnar.

"Come on," he said. "The Land of Ice and Fire awaits you."

Gunnar took a deep breath – and jumped down beside him.

# SEVENTEEN
## THE RAINBOW
# BRIDGE

VIGLAF GOT THE crew to haul the *Sea Eagle* out of the sea and make camp. The beach was narrow, the sand coarse and grey, almost black. A path twisted upwards between tumbled rocks, but mist still clung to the cliff tops and it was impossible to see where it led. Gunnar stood at the bottom looking up.

"Er … forgive me for asking," said Viglaf. "But what's your plan?"

"Leave him alone," said Thorkel. "Can't you see he's thinking?"

"I was only asking," snapped Viglaf. "No need to be so grumpy."

"*Me* grumpy?" said Thorkel. "You're the grumpiest man I know."

Soon they were wrangling again, the crew looking on and laughing. Gunnar tried to block out their voices, but it was impossible. After a while Rurik came over to him. "When in doubt, do anything," said the big man. "That way you'll probably make something happen. Why don't we head inland, you and I?"

"Thanks, Rurik," said Gunnar. "What would I do without you?"

Rurik smiled and they set about preparing for the journey. Thorkel grumbled when he realized he wasn't being invited along, but not much. Viglaf gave them cloaks and some dried fish and flasks of water. He also gave Rurik a byrnie and a sword from the *Sea Eagle*'s weapon chest. At last they were ready.

"Well, take care," said Thorkel. "And don't worry, Viglaf will wait."

Thorkel raised his hand in farewell and they started up the path, Rurik taking the lead. They soon entered the mist, which grew thicker as they climbed. At the top of the cliffs the path disappeared into it a few paces ahead.

Suddenly Gunnar felt a cold breeze stirring and the mist parted as it had done at sea. He heard the beating of wings and harsh cawing, and a pair of ravens flew out of the mist to land in front of them. They cawed again, leaped back into the air and flew off in the direction from where they had come. Gunnar and Rurik turned to each other and grinned. Then they followed the birds.

They walked across empty, rocky country, the ravens just keeping ahead of them. After a while they arrived at a gorge, its entrance flanked by huge stone pillars, and at that moment the sun burned through the mist. Gunnar looked up and was amazed to see a colossal rainbow arching across the sky. One bright end was grounded in the gorge, the other lost in the far distance.

"Bifrost..." said Rurik. "So such a thing really does exist."

"Why of course it does!" said a booming voice, and a red-bearded giant appeared. He wore a shining silver helmet and a silver byrnie that reflected the colours of the rainbow bridge. In one hand he carried a tall spear, its perfect leaf-shaped blade gleaming in the bright light. Gunnar knew this was no mortal.

"You must be Heimdall," he said, remembering what Odin had told him.

"And you must be Gunnar, the boy who wants to visit Valhalla," boomed Heimdall. "Odin told me to keep an eye out for you – and not to stand in your way. He's impatient to see you."

"Your quest is almost over, Gunnar," said Rurik, slapping him on the back. "It won't be long before you're on your way home with your father."

Gunnar smiled and they stepped forward, but

Heimdall barred Rurik's way with his spear. "Only the boy," Heimdall said. "Odin didn't speak of you."

Rurik scowled and half pulled his sword out of its scabbard, ready to fight the God. Gunnar put his hand over Rurik's, stopping him. "Don't worry, Rurik," he said. "I'll be fine. Go back and wait with the others."

"Very well," said Rurik, his eyes still fixed on Heimdall's. Then he turned to Gunnar, his face troubled, as Gunnar remembered it from their night on the drowning posts. "My brother's name was Olaf," said Rurik. "He died bravely, so he might be up there. If you see him, tell him…"

"I will, Rurik," said Gunnar. "So, Heimdall, what do I have to do?"

"Just go to the foot of the rainbow." Heimdall lowered his spear and moved aside. "You'll soon work it out from there."

Gunnar went past him into the gorge, a jagged crevice in the land with rock walls rising on both sides. He walked towards Bifrost, and as he got closer he began to make out the colours blending into each other – red, yellow, green, blue, purple – the whole thing like a giant column of magical, sparkling ice.

He looked back. Rurik was watching intently from the entrance to the gorge, Heimdall next to him. Gunnar carried on until he was less than an arm's length from the bridge. He looked for steps within it, but found nothing. He went closer, took a deep breath ... and touched the rainbow.

His fingertips tingled – and he was pulled inside, then felt himself being flung upwards at incredible speed. He was flying *in* the colours, helpless as an autumn leaf caught in a fast-flowing river, and screaming at the top of his voice.

Then it was over as suddenly as it had begun. Gunnar flew out of the rainbow and rolled over and over until he came to a halt. He lay face down for a moment, gasping for breath, and only raised his head when he heard the sound of ravens cawing. The same two birds were standing in front of him, staring at him with their beady black eyes, their heads cocked to one side.

"Hugin and Munin..." he murmured. "How did *you* get here?"

"They live here, Gunnar," said a voice. "At least

they do when they're not being my eyes and ears. Welcome to Asgard, home of the Gods."

Gunnar looked up. He was on a path that climbed a short, rocky slope. At the top was a great throne carved from stone, and sitting on it was a smiling Odin. He wore a long white robe and was bareheaded, but otherwise he was the same old man Gunnar had met at the God House. Above them the sun was shining in a blue sky, although a pale moon was also visible. The ravens flew to Odin, settling on the throne like sentinels behind him, one on either side.

Gunnar stood for a moment, taking it all in, amazed he was truly *there*. But then he remembered all that had gone before and resentment swelled in his heart. "I suppose I should thank you," he said. "You were generous to me at the God House, and I would have drowned if you hadn't given me that knife in Kaupang. But why did you let it all happen? Why did I have to suffer?"

The ravens squawked, but Odin just laughed. "If I didn't know before that you weren't afraid of anything, I'd know now," he said. "How many other

168

boys would talk to me like that? How many men?"

"You haven't answered my question."

Odin sighed. "I can't control what happens in your world, Gunnar. Skuli was right about man being wolf to man. You mortals do terrible things to one another – always have done, always will. But Rurik was right as well. It is the Norns who weave everyone's fates, even mine. There is no escape from fate."

"So why did you help me?"

"Because you made me an offering of the only precious thing you had." Odin held out a hand – and showed him Father's amulet in his broad palm.

How strange to see it after all this time, Gunnar thought, and to know in whose palm it lay. But how fitting too. His journey had begun with the amulet, and now the journey was ending with it. It seemed his quest *was* over, although he had another question he hardly dared ask. Gunnar raised his eyes to Odin.

"Is my father here?" he said, his voice a whisper. "Can I see him?"

"Turn around, Gunnar," said Odin. "He has been waiting for you."

Gunnar did as he was told. Father was behind him, smiling as he always used to when Gunnar came home to the steading after a day running wild in the forest or out along the Great Fjord. He was dressed as he had been on the night of the hall burning, but there was no bloodstain on his tunic.

"Is it really you, Father?" said Gunnar, his heart leaping.

"Yes, Gunnar," said Father, hugging him. "It's really me."

Gunnar hugged him back, surprised to find himself as tall as Father now. He stood back to look in Father's eyes, then turned to face Odin. "I have one last favour to ask of you," he said. "Will you let my father come home?"

The smile on Odin's face vanished like the sun behind a thunder cloud, and he uttered five words that hit Gunnar like hammer blows.

"No, that can never be."

# EIGHTEEN
# CUTTING
## THE THREADS

FOR A MOMENT Gunnar
was too shocked, too dis-
appointed to speak. "But I
swore on the blood of my
ancestors!" he managed to
splutter at last. "I need Father to come home with
me so he can kill Skuli and Grim and save Mother…"

"*You* swore the oath, Gunnar," said Odin. "So only *you* can fulfil it. To avenge your father's death you will have to kill Skuli in single combat."

"Why didn't you tell me that at the God House?" said Gunnar, his heart filling with anger and resentment again. "You could have saved me a lot of trouble."

"Ah, but you needed the trouble," said Odin. "It was the only way."

"Now you're talking in riddles," said Gunnar. "I don't understand."

"The instant you swore the blood oath you stepped into the world of men," Father explained. "Odin set you on a path that would help you grow up quickly."

"Is that why it had to be so hard? Is that why I had to be a *slave*?"

"I didn't choose that for you, Gunnar," said Odin, shrugging. "It was what happened to you on your journey, that's all. Still, it seems to have worked."

"Odin is right, you're not a boy any more," said Father. "And I'm not just talking about you being

**172**

taller. I've seen what you've done, what you've suffered – Odin showed me everything. You might only be sixteen summers old, Gunnar, but you're braver than most men twice your age. Rurik and Thorkel must think so or they would never have agreed to serve you."

"Even so…" Gunnar said uncertainly. "How can I fight Skuli?"

"I can teach you to be a warrior," Father said. "I always took you hunting with me from the time you learned to walk, so I know you can use a spear. And I showed you something of how to use a sword and shield, if only in games…"

"There are others here who can help you too," said Odin. "Great warriors who sit in Valhalla with little to do, waiting for Ragnarok and wishing they were still alive in the mortal world. When you have learned what you need, you can go back with Rurik and Thorkel and Viglaf and his crew and they can deal with everyone other than Skuli. You would never have met them either if it hadn't been for your journey."

"But all that will take too long, won't it?" said Gunnar.

"Don't worry," said Father. "Your mother is safe for the time being. Skuli pressed her hard to begin with, but she held him off. He said he would give her a year and a day – then marry her whether she liked it or not."

Gunnar looked at him and Odin. Could they really turn him into a warrior in such a short time? They clearly believed it was possible, but Gunnar's heart was still full of doubt. If only he could be sure. If only he could know the future! Then he remembered he was at the top of Yggdrasil, and sitting at the foot of the tree were three beings who had already decided what was to happen.

"All right," he said. "But first I want to ask the Norns about my fate."

"You might not like the answer they give you," said Odin, frowning. He and Father exchanged a look, and Father shrugged as if to say it was fine with him.

"I'll deal with that if I have to," said Gunnar.

"Very well," said Odin. "Close your eyes, Gunnar…"

\* \* \*

Gunnar did as he was told, and when he opened them he was standing before a vast, endless tangle of knotted fibres that pulsed – and he knew that he was looking at the web woven by the Norns. A light flared near by, and Gunnar saw three hunched figures in ragged black cloaks, their skin pale and wrinkled, their mouths toothless and drooling, their hair like nests of snakes. One sat at a huge spindle, new threads spooling off it into the hands of the second, who swiftly wove them into the web, and the third wielded a giant pair of shears.

"Spin and weave, spin and weave," said the first.

"Into a line of silver thread," said the second.

"Then with a little snip … you're dead, dead, dead!" said the third, cutting through several threads at once. The three of them cackled, and Gunnar heard ghostly voices, the spirits of the newly dead wailing softly in the darkness. He wondered who they had been and how they had died. Then all three Norns turned to stare at him, their hands still spinning and weaving and cutting ceaselessly.

"Well, well, well," said the first. "Who have we here?"

"It's the boy," said the second. "Our chosen one!"

"Watching him suffer was so much ... *FUN*!" said the third.

"I'm glad you enjoyed it," he said, returning their gaze. "I came here to ask you a question, but now I have more than one. Why did you choose to make me suffer? And what will my fate be, and that of Skuli?"

"If not you, who else?" said the first, shrugging.

"Too happy, far too blessed!" said the second.

"Definitely in need of a test," said the third, and the cackling began again.

Gunnar sighed. Was that it? He had been too happy, too blessed in his life and parents, so they had decided to take it all away from him? Perhaps it was best never to be happy, then. You couldn't miss what you didn't have. But even as the thought came to him he realized that was no way to live his life.

"You didn't answer my other questions," he said.

"Should we tell him of his fate?" said the first.

"Of course we should!" said the second. "And we won't lie."

"One of you will live," said the third, "and one of you will die!"

Their cackling reached a peak this time, the three of them screaming with laughter. A shimmering pool appeared and cast an eerie, sickly glow. The Norns danced round it, their ragged cloaks and hair flying out around them.

*One of you will live, and one of you will die.* It was hardly a revelation, and there was no comfort in it either. It seemed the only way to find out what lay in the future was to wait until it happened. Odin had been right: he didn't much like their answer. "Thanks for nothing," he said. "How do I get back to Odin?"

The Norns stopped dancing and looked up. Gunnar turned to look in the same direction – and gasped with amazement. The light from the pool showed him the dim outline of an incredible, colossal tree rising into the distant heavens, and he knew it was Yggdrasil, the tree that bore the nine worlds of all creation.

"The boy doesn't like us!" said the first Norn. "What a surprise!"

"He wants to get going," said the second. "And we must get on."

"If he closes his eyes again ..." said the third, "then he'll be gone!"

The instant Gunnar closed his eyes he felt himself flying upwards. He opened his eyes briefly and saw the wonders in Yggdrasil's mighty branches – mountains and seas, forests and cities towering over plains, and the sun and the moon and stars whirling around the great tree like the Norns dancing.

But all he could think of was the coming battle with Skuli.

# NINETEEN
# FATHER
# AND SON

FROM THE OUTSIDE Valhalla appeared to be a large building of turf and logs, no different to any great lord's hall in the world of mortals. But as Gunnar discovered, it was enormous inside, the walls covered in shields and weapons. Crowds of warriors were seated at tables that seemed to go on for ever.

"These are the men who will help us in our work, Gunnar," said Father. "Fine warriors, all of them. They know everything about fighting and war."

Gunnar looked down the lines of men drinking and feasting and talking. His eyes finally snagged on one in particular, a big, broad-shouldered, fair-haired Viking who looked like someone he knew.

"Yes, my name is Olaf," said the young man when Gunnar asked him. "And I have a brother called Rurik…"

They spoke for a while, but Father was keen to start his training. Before long Gunnar was dripping with sweat, his muscles aching from practising with sword and shield and spear. That night he slept next to Father on the floor in Valhalla, and in the morning they went straight out to the training ground again.

The next day was the same, but after that Father began bringing in other warriors to give him fresh challenges and show him that each man's fighting style is his alone. So it went on, Father relentless, pushing Gunnar to the limit and beyond, until one day Gunnar snapped and threw down his sword.

"That's it!" he said, panting. "I can't do this any more. I'm worn out!"

"Pick up your sword, Gunnar," said Father. "You won't be able to ask for a rest when you're fighting Skuli. Not unless you *want* him to kill you."

Gunnar stared at him for a moment. Then he wiped the sweat from his eyes with the back of his hand, picked up the sword, hefted his shield. Soon he and Father were trading blows as before, the sun setting, their long shadows stretching out behind them. "Shield forward, Gunnar," Father said. "Watch my eyes, not my blade. Try a backhand stroke, now parry, that's good…"

The days slipped past, and Gunnar felt himself growing stronger, more at ease with his weapons. But thoughts of Mother and what lay in store for her nagged at him constantly. "Time is running out, Father," he said one day when they were resting. "I'll have to leave soon if I'm to get there in time."

"I know, Gunnar," said Father. "But you're not ready for Skuli yet."

"I might never be ready," Gunnar murmured. "And what happens if Viglaf decides he won't wait for me any more? How will I get home then?"

"I will take you," said a voice. Gunnar turned round and saw Brunhild approaching. Since his arrival in Asgard he had often watched her and the Valkyries bringing dead warriors to Valhalla. She always nodded to him as if they were old friends. But they hadn't spoken. "My wolf can do the journey as swiftly as a thought. That way you can have more time with your father."

"What about Viglaf and the rest?" said Gunnar. "You can't take them all."

"Odin will tell them they should set off now," she said, shrugging.

Gunnar didn't know what to say and stared at her. Father poked him in the shoulder. "Well, that's settled then," said Father. "Now, back to work…"

One morning at the training ground Father produced a bundle, something long and thin wrapped in a wolfskin, and handed it to Gunnar. "Here, you'll need this," he said with a smile. Gunnar quickly unwrapped the bundle, his heart racing, his eyes growing wide when he saw it was Death-Bringer.

He pulled it from the scabbard. Lines of colour writhed in it, cobalt blue and the cold green of sea-soaked wood when it burns and the red of fresh blood. The spiky runes on the blade glowed with new fire.

Gunnar held the sword up to the light, moving it this way and that, swinging it slowly through the air to hear it sing. He thought of the last time he had seen it, tossed on the ground beside Father's corpse, the steel he had loved to polish stained with the blood of four dead Wolf Men. Now that stain was gone, and the steel shone. "Is it truly mine?" he murmured.

"Yes, Gunnar, it's yours. You've more than earned it."

Gunnar lowered the blade. "I won't feel I've earned anything until I fulfil my oath and Skuli lies dead at my feet."

"You know, Gunnar, sometimes I feel like telling you to forget about Skuli." Valhalla loomed over them. "I wish you could go back to the world and just *live* – find a girl, have a son of your own, grow old. We men are stupid with our greed for gold and glory. It's all bloodletting and children left without fathers."

"So why don't you tell me to forget it?" Gunnar said quietly.

"Because you wouldn't listen."

"You're right," said Gunnar. "If I do as you say, Skuli wins. So even if I did have a son I would have to tell him Skuli had his grandfather murdered and took his grandmother for his wife and stole our land – and I did nothing about it. What would he think of me then, Father? What would I think of myself?"

Silence fell between them and they stared at each other. Anyone watching might have said they were more like brothers than father and son. "My answer would have been the same if I had ever been in your position," said Father. "Now, let's see if we can get a bit more work in before this light goes. I might be old, I might even be dead, but I can still teach you a thing or two."

184

\* \* \*

Then one day it was time at last for Gunnar to leave. Brunhild was waiting for him on her wolf. Odin was there with his ravens, the birds cawing. Gunnar's head was suddenly full of all the things he had meant to say, but now he couldn't speak, and his eyes feasted on Father for the last time.

"Take care of yourself, Gunnar," said Father. "And of your mother."

"I will," said Gunnar. He hugged him quickly, and ran to Brunhild, his eyes filling with warm tears that spilled over and ran down his cheeks. She lifted him up to sit in front of her as if he weighed nothing, even though he wore a full chainmail byrnie and an iron helmet, and carried a shield and Death-Bringer in its scabbard on his hip. He gripped the beast's rough pelt with both hands.

"Ready?" said Brunhild. Gunnar nodded and the wolf leaped into the air. As Asgard fell away below them, Gunnar looked back at Father with a hand raised in farewell. They dropped through the sky, diving into Bifrost and out again, then flew over the

Land of Ice and Fire with its mountains, one of them belching flames and smoke. They swooped over the sea and left a trail of white foam in their wake, the glittering wave tops crushed by their passing.

The wind in Gunnar's face was like a living creature, an invisible monster scouring his eyeballs, trying to rip him from the wolf. But he hung on, and before long he saw the land rushing to meet them. His heart leapt as he realized they were flying into the Great Fjord, its steep, stony sides wrapping round him like an embrace. And there, drawn up on the small, rocky beach at the head of the fjord was the *Sea Eagle*, Rurik and Thorkel waiting beside it, both in helmet and byrnie and armed with sword and shield.

# TWENTY
# STORM OF
# BLADES

GUNNAR JUMPED DOWN from the flying wolf. Thorkel stared at Brunhild and her mount, his mouth open, ready to take to his heels. But Rurik laughed. He ran up to Gunnar and flung an

187

arm round his shoulders.

"You see, Thorkel!" said Rurik. "I told you he'd come!"

"You did tell me, Rurik," said Thorkel. "Over and over again."

"Where's Viglaf?" said Gunnar. "I thought he'd be with you."

"I am," whispered a voice from inside the *Sea Eagle*. "But I'm not coming out until that creature has gone." Viglaf was nervously peering at Brunhild and her great beast from between two shields on the ship's side.

"The rest of his lads are hiding in the woods," said Rurik, grinning.

"I can't blame them," muttered Thorkel. "I might join them soon."

"You won't have to," said Rurik. "I think she's about to leave."

Gunnar looked round and saw that he was right. "It is time to say farewell, Gunnar Bjornsson," said Brunhild. Her wolf snorted as if it were saying farewell too. "I wish you strength in your sword arm and luck in the coming storm of blades. And I hope it will be many years before you ride with me again."

Brunhild and her wolf rose into the pale sky and swiftly flew away down the fjord. She looked round at Gunnar once, and then she was gone.

Gunnar sat by a driftwood fire and caught up with what had happened to his friends. It seemed that Odin himself had appeared in their camp and told them to set off. They had reached the fjord that very morning, and Rurik had already taken a scouting party up to the woods above the steading.

"Skuli has had your hall rebuilt," he said. "There are a few scorch marks on the walls, but it's got a new roof that probably keeps the rain out."

"Did you see him?" said Gunnar.

"Big man with a black beard? Struts around like he thinks he's important?" said Thorkel. Gunnar nodded. "We saw him."

"We also saw plenty of fighting men," said Rurik. "Some who didn't look as if they'd be much of a problem. Some who did."

So Skuli had brought in more of his warriors, as

well as Grim and his Wolf Men. "How many men do you think he has altogether?" Gunnar asked.

"Thirty, maybe a few more," said Rurik. "So with Viglaf and his lads I think we're evenly matched. There was a lot going on, though."

"Rurik's right," said Thorkel. "The kind of hustle and bustle you see on a steading when it's being prepared for some kind of special occasion."

"Like for a wedding?" said Gunnar, his blood running cold. Rurik and Thorkel glanced at each other. "Did you see my mother?"

"No, I don't think so," Rurik said, his voice gentle. "If Skuli does intend to marry her, I'd guess he wouldn't let her out of the hall."

"So it's today, a year and a day since the hall was burned down…" said Gunnar.

"Well then," said Thorkel, breaking into his thoughts. "What's the plan?"

"We take back my steading," Gunnar said grimly. "And I kill Skuli."

"Spoken like a man," said Rurik, clapping him on the shoulder.

But Gunnar still didn't feel like a man, however hard he tried.

They climbed the path into the woods an hour after sunset, thirty men in chainmail, starlight glinting off their helmets, their weapons quietly chinking, the dead leaves of autumn rustling under their iron-shod boots. After a while they reached the edge of the forest and looked down at the steading.

"I don't like it," whispered Viglaf. "We might be walking into a trap."

"What do you think, Gunnar?" said Rurik. "Is Skuli expecting you?"

"I doubt it," said Gunnar, remembering the way Skuli had spoken to him. "I'd be surprised if he's given me a moment's thought since the night I left."

"That's good enough for me," said Rurik. "Let's go!"

He ran down the slope, the rest following, a wave of warriors heading for the gate in a silent rush. Gunnar kept up but couldn't help wondering why Viglaf and Thorkel stayed just in front of him and Erlend so close behind. They were behaving like body-guards, and Gunnar realized they still thought of him as a boy, someone they needed to protect. And why should they think anything else? They had never seen him fight, after all.

Not that he had ever fought properly. He knew how to hold his sword and shield, felt comfortable in his chainmail, had learned the lessons of those practice sessions with Father in Valhalla. But that's all they had ever been – practice, not the real thing. He had never stood toe to toe with a warrior who knew how to kill him. Suddenly his new confidence began to drain away.

They reached the gate and Rurik led them in. A couple of Wolf Men were standing just inside, warming themselves at a brazier. They took one look at the armed men approaching and ran for their lives. "To arms! We're under attack!" they yelled, and Rurik grinned. "That should wake everyone up," he said.

By the time they got to the longhouse men were pouring out of it, pulling on chainmail, fumbling with their weapons, helmets askew. Gunnar wasn't sure what he had expected to happen next, but it was shocking in its swiftness. Rurik sprinted forward, screaming a war cry. His blade flashed in the torchlight and he cut down two Wolf Men before they could raise their shields.

Thorkel and Viglaf made short work of several more, then Gunnar was in the thick of it, a Wolf Man raining blows on his shield. Around him blades rose and fell, spears jabbed and snapped, men grunted and yelled and screamed and died. Gunnar gasped for breath, his shield heavy on his arm. A Wolf Man swung an axe at him and he ducked, the blade swishing just over his head. He raised Death-Bringer, but Erlend stepped forward and cut the Wolf Man down.

"Don't worry, Gunnar, we'll take care of you!" said Erlend, grinning at him. The Wolf Man's blood was spattered over Erlend's cheek and chest.

"But I don't *want* you to take care of me!" Gunnar yelled.

Erlend, however, was fighting, not listening. Before long most of the Wolf Men were dead, and those who were still alive turned and fled, keen to save their skins. But half a dozen warriors stood shoulder to shoulder in front of the longhouse door, their shields overlapping and swords raised.

Gunnar recognized them as the men who had been with Skuli when he had first come to the steading. They had killed several of Viglaf's crew in the fighting, including Einar Squint-Eye. Now they stared at Rurik and Thorkel and Viglaf and the others, who stared back at them from behind their own shields.

"All right, lads," said Thorkel. "If you yield now, I'll ask the true lord of this steading if he'll spare your lives. Or you can die. It's up to you."

True lord of the steading? Gunnar realized that was him. Skuli's warriors said nothing, and the only sound beneath the dark sky was that of torch flames flapping and hissing. Then the shield wall parted and Gunnar saw Grim's archers, arrows notched in their bows, and Grim himself drawing his sword.

"They seem to have made their minds up, Gunnar," said Rurik.

Gunnar saw that Grim was surprised by the mention of his name, and that now the Wolf Men's chief

194

was studying him with a puzzled expression. Gunnar smiled, then nodded at Rurik – and the bloodletting began again.

# TWENTY-ONE
# FIGHT
## TO THE DEATH

THE FIGHTING ROUND the long-house door was hard and bitter. Thorkel and Rurik soon cut down Grim and the archers, although not before a couple more of Viglaf's crew had been killed, one with an arrow in his throat, the other with

196

Grim's sword in his chest. Skuli's men exacted a tough price for their lives too, killing three more of Viglaf's crew. But at last they lay dead as well. Gunnar stepped over the bodies, and entered the hall with Rurik beside him, their boots sticky with blood.

A fire burned in the hearth. Long tables bore jugs of ale and mead and great platters of food. Thick swags of holly had been hung on the walls and pine branches nailed to the rafters as decoration. The people of the farm were sitting on the benches, all quite terrified. They must have heard the sounds of battle outside, and now Gunnar had burst in, a warrior in chainmail and helmet with his sword drawn, a band of armed Vikings rushing in behind him.

Skuli and Mother were on the other side of the hearth. Skuli held her by the arm, his fingers digging into her flesh. But her face glowed with joy.

"Welcome home, Gunnar," she said, trying to pull away from Skuli. "Your father told me everything in a dream. You look more like him than ever."

"Be quiet, woman," snarled Skuli. "Gunnar was a

197

snot-nosed brat who ran off a year ago and probably got eaten by wolves in the forest. This is some young adventurer you've cooked up a plot with. It's all lies."

"I ran off because at the time I had no choice," Gunnar said quietly. "But I swore a blood oath that night, Skuli – and I've returned to fulfil it."

"Is that so?" said Skuli, sneering. "Even if it's true, you obviously realized you're not up to it. Otherwise why would you need a band of hired killers?"

"They came to even up the odds and make it a fair battle," Gunnar said. "Now it's just between you and me. Draw your sword and we'll finish it."

"You want a fight to the death?" said Skuli. Gunnar nodded. "Don't make me laugh," Skuli went on. "If I win, your men will cut me down anyway."

"And I will if they don't," said Mother, shooting him a look of hatred.

Skuli whipped out his dagger and held it against her throat, pulling her to him. She struggled, but he was too strong. "I'm beginning to think I don't want to marry you after all," he hissed. "I'd be forever looking over my shoulder."

"Let her go," said Gunnar. Rurik and Thorkel stepped forward, their blades raised. Viglaf and his men muttered and pushed up behind them.

"One step closer and I'll slit her throat from ear to ear," growled Skuli, pressing the edge of the dagger harder into Mother's pale skin.

"Stop!" yelled Gunnar, and nobody moved. "What do you want?"

"I know if I kill her I'm a dead man, but I'll trade you her life for a promise. Make your men swear they won't harm me whatever happens, and I'll let her live – and I'll fight you as well. I can't be fairer than that, can I?"

"Don't do it, Gunnar," said Mother, her voice pleading. "Kill him even if it means I have to die too! You're all that matters – I want you to live…"

Thorkel moved so Skuli couldn't see his face and whispered to Gunnar. "Tell him what he wants to hear and we'll kill him as soon as he lets her go."

"Forget your oath," said Rurik. "You were a boy when you swore it…"

Gunnar listened, their voices filling his head, but

then he pushed them both out of his way and looked straight into Skuli's eyes. "I agree," he said. "Let her go. No one will harm you if you kill me."

"Are you sure, Gunnar?" said Rurik. Thorkel frowned.

"I've never been more sure of anything, Rurik," said Gunnar. "Now swear, everyone!" he yelled. "No one is to harm Skuli, whatever happens!"

There was more muttering, but they all swore. Skuli released Mother and she ran to Gunnar. He dropped his shield and they held each other. Mother's tears were wet on his cheek. "You're thinner, Mother," he said.

"And you're bigger," she said, stepping back to look at him.

"So, how are we going to do this?" said Skuli. "Viking rules, I trust?"

Rurik and Thorkel exchanged a look. "What does he mean?" Gunnar asked.

"No helmet or byrnie, stripped to the waist, swords only," murmured Rurik, his face grim. "No quarter, and you fight to the last drop of blood."

"Fine by me," said Gunnar. "Help me get my byrnie off, Rurik."

Thorkel ordered a space to be cleared while Gunnar and Skuli got ready. Viglaf and his men turned over the tables and pushed them back against the walls, dashing platters and jugs to the floor in the process. Before long the hall was quiet, torches burning brightly, a silent ring of faces waiting for the fight to begin, the people of the farm mixed in with Viglaf's crew.

"Can we get on with it now?" said Skuli at last, impatience in his voice.

Gunnar turned to look at him. Skuli stood on the other side of the hearth, the pale white skin of his broad shoulders gleaming in the torchlight. His deep chest was covered in a mat of black hair, the same texture as his beard, and unlike some men he seemed bigger without his tunic on, almost as if the power in him had been unleashed. Gunnar felt naked and vulnerable and afraid.

Skuli was holding his sword, and now he raised it for some practice swings. Torchlight flared off the blade as it sliced through the air, humming and whistling. Gunnar watched the play of muscles in Skuli's arm and chest, Skuli swinging his sword faster and faster until it was almost a blur.

"Very pretty," Rurik called out. "But it doesn't mean you can fight."

Other voices jeered, Thorkel and Viglaf and the people of the farm beginning to yell. "We'll soon see about that, won't we?" said Skuli, grinning.

Gunnar felt the eyes of everyone turn to look at him, and he swallowed, his throat suddenly dry and painful. Mother kissed his cheek and moved aside, her face pale, tears flowing once more. Rurik squeezed his shoulder and said something about keeping his guard up. Thorkel's mouth was moving but Gunnar couldn't hear him. The crowd was baying now, Erlend's voice rising above the others, yelling, "Good luck, Gunnar, give him all you've got!" and then Gunnar found himself moving towards Skuli, Death-Bringer raised.

Skuli laughed and sprang forward, aiming a blow at his head. Gunnar brought Death-Bringer up and their blades clanged together, the shock travelling up Gunnar's arm. Then Skuli went low, slicing at Gunnar's legs, trying to chop him down. Gunnar blocked that stroke, and another, retreating as Skuli came on, still laughing, enjoying himself. Gunnar stumbled and almost fell and Rurik yelled at him, "Stay on your feet! Don't let him corner you!"

Gunnar was panting, sweat streaming off him. Skuli was backing him towards a corner of the hall, but there seemed to be nothing he could do about it. Skuli was hammering at him, stroke after stroke, Gunnar desperately holding him off, the sound of metal clanging on metal ringing in his head, Father's training forgotten. Then Skuli began to talk, making fun of him.

"So this is Gunnar, the hero who went to Valhalla a boy and came back a man... Well, as far as I can see you're still a boy ... a little boy trying to be a man, holding his father's sword when he should be playing with toys..."

The old doubts filled Gunnar, and he wondered how he could ever have hoped to beat a grown man, a warrior like Skuli. But then he parried one of Skuli's

blows – and struck one of his own, almost knocking Skuli's sword from his hand. Skuli frowned. Suddenly Gunnar knew that he *was* a man, whatever Skuli might say, and the doubts vanished like mist burned by the sun.

Rurik and Thorkel yelled encouragement as Gunnar pushed forward, striking again, getting into a rhythm. Soon Death-Bringer was singing and Skuli no longer laughed. He chopped and hacked at Gunnar, attacking him from every angle. But now it was Gunnar who was relentless, parrying every stroke, wielding his blade as Father had taught him, forcing his enemy back. Skuli looked at him through their whirling blades, his eyes haunted.

They stamped through the hearth, kicking up a shower of sparks. They swept towards a wall, people scattering out of their way like chickens frightened by two dogs fighting in a farmyard. At last Skuli broke off and yelled, "Stop!"

"No quarter," Gunnar said. "Viking rules, remember?"

"Forget the rules," said Skuli, his chest heaving.

"I'll make you an offer. I can give you power and wealth. Don't turn me down like your fool of a father."

"My father was no fool," said Gunnar. "And neither am I."

Gunnar closed his eyes and saw the third Norn holding her shears over a thick thread. He heard all three sisters cackling. *One will live and one will die...* Then he opened his eyes and swung Death-Bringer for the last time in this fight. The blade swept clean through Skuli's neck and his head rolled across the floor.

Gunnar raised Death-Bringer in triumph, and torchlight leaped from it like bolts of lightning. *"GUNNAR! GUNNAR!"* roared the people of his hall.

This was his home, and no man would ever take it from him again.